JERK BAIT

a novel by

MIA SIEGERT

For information on subsidiary rights, please contact the publisher at rights@jollyfishpress.com. For more information about the book, please visit our website at www.jollyfishpress.com, or write us at Jolly Fish Press, PO Box 1773, Provo, UT 84603-1773.

Printed in the United States of America

THIS TITLE IS ALSO AVAILABLE AS AN EBOOK.

Library of Congress Cataloging-in-Publication Data is available.

ISBN 978-1-631630-66-8

10 9 8 7 6 5 4 3 2 1

For my family and friends.

Praise for *Jerkbait*

"Every athlete, parent and high school kid, gay or straight, will see some of themselves reflected in *Jerkbait's* teammates and families. So will every ally who wants to see change. *Jerkbait* is gutsy, urgent, raw and hopeful." —Brian Kitts, co-founder, You Can Play.

"*Jerkbait* was an excellent read on the complex issues facing LBGTQ athletes, as well as their families, featuring complex, believable characters who would not be out of place in any high school across America." —Chris Kluwe, former NFL player, LGBTQ rights activist, and author of *Prime*

"*Jerkbait* is an intriguing look into the world of both parents and kids as they try to navigate the difficult path to the draft. A cautionary tale and a must-read for parents and kids alike." —Patrick O'Sullivan, former NHL player, child safety advocate, and author of *Breaking Away: A Harrowing True Story of Resilience, Courage, and Triumph*

"Mia Siegert's poignant, vibrant first novel deals with issues of sexual orientation, which makes it very timely, and with issues of the human heart, which makes it timeless." —Mark Spencer, award-winning author of *A Haunted Love Story: The Ghosts of the Allen House*

"Poignant in the real sense: sharply drawn, pointed, and piercing." —David Galef, award-winning author of *How to Cope with Suburban Stress*

"From beginning to end, this book was explosive." —Nicole Tone, *This Literary Life*

"Electric and explosive, yet soft and nuanced, *Jerkbait* is a powerhouse of a debut that is bound to leave a mark on the world of YA lit." —Laurie Elizabeth Flynn, author of *Firsts*

"What is arguably the most important aspect of Siegert's work, however, is the spotlight it throws on the plight of gay athletes, particularly at the high school level. In an environment where the performance of masculinity is tangled up with a million other bits of codified repressive social behavior, and where teen boys police each other ruthlessly and sometimes violently, the risk of depression and self-harm is excruciatingly high. I sincerely hope that this book finds its way into the hands of every gay high school athlete, so that they might know they are not alone." —Caleb Roehig, author of *Last Seen Leaving*

JERKBAIT

a novel

MIA SIEGERT

JOLLY
FISH
PRESS
Provo, Utah

1

My twin Robbie tried to die.

I guess he had since day one. My first breath was fourteen minutes after Robbie's. He came out breach—sudden, fast, and hard—moments before Mom could be pulled in for an emergency C-section, and broke her tailbone on the way out. I came out the right way. Unmemorable, like on holidays when Mom and Dad would drink too much and tell stories about how awful it was when Robbie was born, but not even mention how I came out of the same womb just after.

I'd been walking unnoticed in Robbie's flattened path ever since. Those fourteen minutes stayed between us like a wall. Me on the side with the shadow. I didn't have to think about him except when the debris of his destruction lobbed over and caught me in the face. We were two countries; no shared thoughts, languages, customs. We weren't at all alike; we just happened to have been alive in this vast world for almost exactly the same amount of time.

And in the rare instances we were forced to sit together, our lungs matched up. Our singular twin party trick. I wasn't thinking about this as I plied through pain in my room. Robbie was far away from this part of my life. *Breathe in*—I lowered my foot to first position—*breathe out*—I dipped into the first *plié relevé*. A sudden tightness wrapped around my stomach, like someone was clenching it in hard pulses. It thudded in my ears too quickly, the noise drowning out the instructions from the YouTube video. Nausea rose to my esophagus.

For the first time in my life, I felt what Robbie must have felt during those first fourteen minutes. I was breathing alone. And I knew exactly where he was. Like there had never been a wall.

I yanked off my headphones and staggered out of my room toward the bathroom we shared. The door was shut. Through it I could hear the sound of the shower.

I pounded on it. "Robbie, need to use the bathroom."

There was no response. My face wrinkled. I banged on the door until it rattled. "Robbie, stop jerking off. Gonna be sick."

There was a sound, something muffled and garbled, and a thud.

I turned to the stairs and hesitated. With everything turning on its side, it was more likely I'd fall down the steps and break my neck. I pounded on the door again. "Robbie, seriously, open up!"

Still nothing.

Screw it.

With a growl, I twisted the knob, almost tripping when the door swung in, banging against something that prevented it from opening completely. I squeezed through the small gap and my skin turned to ice.

Robbie was curled on the floor, fully dressed and trembling, his bleached hair dry despite the running shower. He clutched his hands over his mouth. His fingers were swollen, throat expanding and contracting like a bullfrog as he gagged. Vomit leaked through his fingers onto the tile, frothy and white.

SUICIDE ATTEMPT, they called it.

I called it bullshit.

He probably just wanted to get high, like he did with the guys after we won a game. Like he did with the guys after we lost one. Off-season, at parties, on the roof.

We went to pick him up on Monday, three days after the EMTs pried us apart, at first unable to tell who the victim was; we were both covered in vomit. Robbie's vomit. I was shaking; Robbie was still as death.

"You've been pretty quiet, Tristan."

I met Mom's eyes in the rearview mirror of the SUV. Her lips were in a taut, red line. Always Revlon, Certainly Red. Dad's hands gripped the steering wheel so tightly his knuckles were white. I waited to see if she was serious before softly answering, "Nothing to say." Sometimes with Mom, it was hard to tell.

"You really don't have any questions about it?"

I should have said no. That's what Dad had trained us to say over the past eighteen years, just like with everything else. *You need to be prepared for interviews. Don't give anything to the press. Hide your cards.* Mom didn't much like questions either. Not unless she was asking them. And even then, she usually didn't want an answer.

But still, I asked, "Why'd he do it?"

Dad's dark eyes caught mine in the rearview mirror—a silent "you should know better." My lips snapped together. Dad was right; I did know better.

"Robbie didn't do anything." Each enunciated syllable made me shiver. "Understood?"

I swallowed and nodded.

"When Coach Benoit asks you what happened, what do you tell him?"

"Nothing?"

Dad pulled into the Mountainside Hospital parking lot. He parked the car and undid his seatbelt. "Food poisoning," he said. "You tell him it was food poisoning."

He stepped out of the car. I unbuckled my seatbelt and grabbed the handle just as Dad hit the lock button with the clicker. Through the closed door he loudly said, "I'll get him myself."

We watched him cross the parking lot. Mom slouched in her seat. Only when Dad was inside the building did I ask, "Should we really be picking him up this early?"

"There's a game on Saturday," Mom answered. "You know that."

"Yeah, but—"

"But what, Tristan?" Mom turned around in her seat to face me. "You think he's going to get drafted if he sits out a game as a healthy scratch?"

I waited to see if Mom wanted me to answer. She turned her attention to her iPhone. Guess not. I'm not sure if I would have known what to say anyway. Maybe suggest that Robbie *wasn't* healthy.

I looked out the window. Had the situation been different, I might have enjoyed watching the flow of people who stayed around hospitals. It would have been perfect for a character study. So many different types of people slipped in and out of the hospital's sliding doors. Decrepit old people creeping on walkers, middle-aged lawyers in suits, crying snot-faced children, fat nurses on a smoke break—all people who looked like they belonged in a hospital. All unhappy people. All people who could have considered suicide.

Robbie didn't belong here. He hadn't seemed depressed, at least no more than any other senior. Everyone in high school was depressed to some degree no matter the grade. Stress from classes, cliques, extracurricular crap, SATs, college acceptances, college rejections, wait lists—it added up. High school was a time for everyone to be miserable.

It wasn't a suicide attempt. He tried to get high. That was the only explanation my brain would accept.

As we waited, I softly murmured the song "All That's Known" from Spring Awakening. I rarely sang around anyone, let alone my parents, but Mom was absorbed with her iPhone. If she noticed, it was close enough to a rock song that I could simply say one of the guys played it at practice and that I couldn't get it out of my head. My best friend Heather often asked me why I never told my parents I wanted to act professionally. She didn't get that I already had a role to play.

When Mom found out she was pregnant with twins, Dad actually wept. At the time, everyone was making a fuss over the Sedins, identical twins, now some of the best forwards in the NHL. Dad envisioned that for Robbie and me, but in his head we'd play for the New Jersey Devils. They were the only team that ever invited Dad to training camp, before he got too many concussions to continue in the ECHL as an enforcer and got his certificate from the NHLPA to be an agent—*our* agent—doing everything he could to sign his clients, including us, with the Devils. It didn't matter that Lou Lamoriello was no longer the general manager after a twenty-seven-year tenure; Dad was loyal to that team and would be until the day he died. Robbie adopted that allegiance and dreamed of being drafted by the Devils, although he'd gladly wear any seal if it meant being in the league.

I didn't dream of hockey. I never did. Maybe I would have if I weren't always compared to Robbie. Instead, I dreamed of a Broadway stage and dancing. Of singing show tunes and making the audience *feel*. Of being a star, taking the final bow at curtain call.

I'd never be a hockey star. At least not like Robbie, whom scouts had drooled over since we were ten. Definitely not like Robbie, who skated effortlessly, feet so light Coach Benoit sometimes called him Twinkle Toes (which actually was a compliment) or Gretzky 2.0 (which made Robbie incoherent).

Squinting across the lot, I could see Dad and Robbie emerge from the sliding doors. Robbie didn't look pale, or sick. He seemed normal, every inch the promising draft pick he was projected to be: tall with broad shoulders and plenty of time to fill out. He already had ten pounds over my one-sixty-five. That would soon change to twenty—maybe twenty-five—of hard, solid muscle.

Robbie climbed in the backseat. He scratched the rip in his jeans, flashing me a smile like we were leaving hockey practice instead of the hospital. He wasn't some skinny kid with a *My Little Pony* shirt and slashed up wrists. Obnoxious, smiling jocks didn't try to kill themselves on leftover Percocet, especially not when they were going to be draft-eligible at the end of the season.

But they might accidentally overdose on leftover Percocet because they thought it'd give them a nice drug ride. Stupid.

I thought maybe I'd feel sick, or depressed, or maybe even the sympathy that family members were supposed to have for their loved ones, but I felt nothing. At least nothing nice. It was hard to think positive from my resident spot in his shadow. Robbie took after Dad, sometimes beating the crap out of me if I made a mistake that cost us a game. But eventually, his fists stopped. Eventually, he realized I just couldn't do what he could. That was almost worse.

As we pulled out of the Mountainside Hospital parking lot, an ambulance whizzed past us in the opposite direction. Its sirens wailed, lights flashing blue and red. I imagined Robbie strapped to a gurney getting his stomach pumped and shuddered. I should have been on the ambulance with him but the EMTs left me behind.

"You okay, Tristan?" Robbie asked, touching my shoulder with the tips of his hard fingers, like I was the one who overdosed. I froze. Robbie offering a gentle touch rather than a harsh shove was weird, even though he hadn't really hit me in about a year. Lately, what I'd get was silence. Not the mute sort of silent, but the kind where people talked without saying anything at all.

But that'd mean the EMT was definitely right, that it was intentional. That it wasn't my twin failing at getting high, but something a lot more permanent, irreversible. Something that a normal twin should have picked up on a long time ago.

But we weren't normal twins. And even though I shivered, nodded, and bit the inside of my cheek, I still felt nothing.

2

Once we arrived back home after a stop at McDonald's—Robbie's favorite place to get a cheat meal—Robbie started to jog up the stairs, slurping his shake. Before he could get halfway up, Dad's voice boomed, "Robbie. Dining room. *Now.*" As I tried to slink against the wall to make my escape, he added, "You too, Tristan."

Great. I hated family pow-wows. Dad always talked about *us* needing to be responsible, and by *we*, he meant Robbie. I was just guilty by proxy.

Robbie groaned and thudded back down the steps. He dropped onto the living room couch, half-draped over the arm. Then he pulled out his salad from the bag, opened the container, and squeezed dressing all over his lettuce. My cheeseburger was still untouched and my fries were barely picked at. Dad always flipped out whenever we ate in the living room with its cream-carpeted floors and furniture. I waited for him to tell Robbie to put the container away, but Dad said nothing. My twin took a bite and chewed with an open mouth as if daring Dad to say anything. I was kind of surprised. It'd been awhile since he really challenged Dad.

I sat on the opposite side of the couch from Robbie. The coffee table separated us from our parents. It wasn't a broad enough barrier.

Mom looked at Dad, then began, "Your father and I have decided that you two are going to be sharing a room."

"Huh?"

Sharing a bedroom? Our rooms weren't even twelve square feet after our parents remodeled and enlarged the bathroom so it'd have a jacuzzi, shower, and small infrared sauna in case Robbie's muscles tightened up. Although tiny, my room was my safe space. It was where I could put on headphones and write, learn choreography, and use my desk for barre work. I could turn on a fan and press a pillow to my face to mute my singing. It was where I'd steer clear from Robbie whenever he missed the game-winning goal in a shoot out, or the Devils lost to the Rangers or something. He could get really ugly then, flipping over furniture, screaming, punching walls, and sometimes me. Especially if we lost a game because *I* made a mistake and *then* the Devils lost to the Rangers in overtime in a playoff game.

Robbie chewed then swallowed a cherry tomato. "You know, we're eighteen. Not eight. Just in case you forgot."

Dad's face hardened. "Eighteen or not, you're under our roof. No different than away games."

Robbie looked at me then jerked his chin toward Mom and Dad. In spite of our general lack of non-verbal twin language, I could practically hear him saying, *Come on, do something.*

I took a deep breath. It was my turn on the defense stand. Older twin, younger twin. Last resort twin.

"I'm, uh—" I paused to clear my throat. "I'm not really sure why you're punishing us."

"We're not punishing you. We need to keep an eye on you two," Mom said.

Before I could stop myself, I blurted out, "But Robbie was the one who tried to kill himself, not me."

I could hear my sudden heartbeat in my ears. Envisioned Dad tackling me to the ground, hands squeezing around my throat as Mom begged him to knock it off. My shoulders trembled. I stared at the carpet like it would soften the blow of Dad's fists but couldn't help glancing up at him just once. Dad's hands were bunched. "Food poisoning," he said hoarsely. "It was food poisoning. Understood?"

"Yes, sir," Robbie and I mumbled, our voices joining in rare unison.

Dad got to his feet and walked out of the living room. Our meeting was over. The couch cushions gave when Robbie stood up. I heard him jog up the stairs, the quiet creak of a door opening, then the loud bang of it shutting. I wondered which room he entered, which one we'd be sharing. Had Mom and Dad brought in the futon or would one of us have to sleep on the floor in a sleeping bag? I didn't want to sleep on the floor, or the futon, but Robbie would get first dibs. Suicide aside, he always did.

I stood up with my food and walked to the stairs. Mom touched my arm before I could take the first step. The only time she ever initiated physical contact was whenever she made an excuse for Robbie. Starved as I was for attention, her touches were never for my sake, so I pulled away.

She took a deep breath. "Can we talk?"

I looked at my McDonald's bag and cup of Coke. It was harder to smell the aroma of meat and fatty grease from the bag. The ice had probably melted by now, and the burger was probably cold. Maybe we'd get food poisoning for real. Joke's on you, Dad.

"I know this is frustrating for you in particular," she said shakily, as if she forgot her lines. I didn't know why she bothered. Any time Robbie got in trouble, I wasn't allowed to go out either. Dad said it was because I was the responsible twin, that it was my duty to keep an eye on Robbie, keep him from sneaking out, drinking with teammates, and smoking weed on the roof. Whether Mom agreed didn't matter; she also didn't argue.

I knew my line. "What do you need me to do?"

Mom rubbed her forehead, French tip fingernails sliding into her hair. "The medicine cabinet is to be kept empty. If Robbie needs a pain killer, you're to get it for him and mark the drug, dose, and time. You're to check the room every day before school, when you get home, and before bed. If you find anything, you're to bring it to me immediately. Understood?"

Mom folded her arms, waiting for me to tell her I understood my brother was going to live out Dad's failed dream no matter what. Sometimes I wonder what Dad's plans were for me. I was good enough for our high school hockey team, but on scouting depth charts, I was embarrassingly low, "probably not draftable." Unlike Robbie who might even be a late first-rounder depending on the draft combine in June.

"What about after wins?" I asked. We always had parties after wins, the guys rotating who'd host. Robbie always went, but usually I went to Heather's instead. Nothing wrong with my teammates, and there would always be an open invite for me, but we had nothing in common outside of hockey. They got along so well with Robbie because he was interested in nothing *but* hockey.

"You can surely spend a few hours with him and his friends."

Right. *His* friends. So much for Heather and the rest of *my* friends, who admittedly were only my friends because of Heather. But still. Thanks, Mom.

With a reluctant nod, I padded up the stairs. Robbie's

door was open. I peered in. The room was empty except for his desk and hockey posters, mostly of the Devils, especially his favorite, Adam Henrique. That meant we'd be staying in my room. I wondered when our parents even had the time to rearrange everything. Did they hire someone to help them while I was at school before we went to pick him up?

I returned to my room, took a deep breath, and opened my door. I almost screamed.

My bed was gone. In its place, a bunk bed. A friggin' *bunk bed*. What. The. Hell. On the opposite side of the room sat a long, plastic table instead of my desk. There were two rolling chairs there, one already occupied by Robbie, along with our iMacs, and a wireless printer in between them. Stiffly, I set my bag of McDonalds and Coke next to my computer and sat down.

Robbie turned in his chair to face me. I stared at the screen so I wouldn't have to look at him.

"I'm sorry," he muttered.

I unwrapped my cheeseburger and took a bite. Barely warm, with hardening yellow American cheese, gross. My Coke was watery, barely flavored. Even grosser.

"No, really. Tristan, I'm sorry." His voice sounded sincere, so similar to mine it could have been a recording.

I swiveled around on my computer chair. Robbie clenched his hat in his hands. There was a good inch of brown roots in his ear-length bleached hair, the same color as mine. "Just wanted you to know that."

I knew it then, with startling clarity and absolute certainty: Robbie wasn't trying to get high. He intentionally tried to die.

Then Robbie got up, walked to the bunk bed, and climbed up the ladder. "I call top."

I opened my mouth but then shut it. I didn't want the

top bunk anyway, not that I wanted a freaking bunk bed or to share my room. Being his roommate for away games was bad enough with all of his pranks—bucket of ice water propped on the door, wedging Dubble Bubble gum in the fingers of my gloves, unscrewing the lid on my Gatorade bottle. Even though it'd been more than a year since the last time he punched me, if I pissed him off, I'd have no place to escape. "It's just hormones," Mom had said the one time I complained after Robbie slammed me into the boards at practice just to call me a loser in front of everyone. "He's under a lot of stress," she said another time as she iced the purple bruising around my eye.

How long would we have to share my room? Probably a few days, a week at most before Robbie fussed enough to get his room back, using some sort of bullshit excuse about it affecting his play.

I picked at a French fry. I knew my role: be a good son to my parents, try to ignore Robbie, and do what was requested of me. Just had to share my room, for now, and keep thinking about the future.

The second I graduated, I'd be gone. No looking back. I'd never told anyone about my plan, not even Heather. I'd maintain a great GPA so I could get a full ride to a good performing arts college like NYU. I'd graduate and get on Broadway, Off-Broadway, or at least a national tour.

I'd get away from my clueless parents, away from my identical stranger—my new roommate I didn't know at all despite nine months together in the womb, head to toe, yin-yang. I'd get a stage name. A strange name. Nothing that could tie me to the Betterby family. I'd be reborn into a world without our biased parents. And most importantly, without being the shadow of Robbie.

3

When I approached Heather's locker on Friday morning, she had crazy pink streaks in her hair. Last week, they were teal. She always went a bit nuts with her looks whenever she wasn't auditioning. Every few months, her private vocal teacher insisted that she take some time off so she wouldn't wreck her voice. "Way too young to have your career cut short," she'd say as she smoked a cigarette on a stick.

"Hey, Tristan," she greeted, turning to show me an *Attack on Titan* backpack. "Like my new swag?"

"I thought you said you weren't into anime anymore."

"Yeah, well, this show's different. It's *good*."

"Uh huh." I fiddled with the clip on my messenger bag, thumb brushing over the thirty pins on the front, one for every team in the NHL. Something my dad insisted Robbie and I do.

Heather closed her locker. "What's wrong?"

"Hm?"

"You're barely looking at me."

"Just a lot on my mind."

"Like?"

I bit the inside of my cheek. "I'm not supposed to talk about it."

"Wooooow. You're going there?" Heather's nose wrinkled. "How long have I been your best friend?"

"Please don't do that."

"Four years." She touched my bicep. "You *know* whatever it is will stay just between us."

"It's not about me, though."

She quirked her brow. "Robbie?"

My thumb snagged on the Toronto Maple Leafs pin. I barely could meet her eye. "He tried to kill himself."

Heather barely got her hand over her mouth before she could gasp out loud. "Oh my God, are you serious? When? Why would he do that?"

"Few days ago, and I don't know." I shifted my weight. "My parents are making me keep an eye on him. Check for prescriptions and whatnot. They even put a bunkbed in my room and are making us share."

"A *bunkbed?* What are you, five?"

"Apparently."

Heather frowned. "I'd say that sucks, but looking on the bright side, I guess it's nice they trust you, right?"

"This has nothing to do with trust. They just can't risk their NHL superstar getting hurt, God forbid they send him to a therapist."

"Why won't they send him to one?"

"It's really stupid."

"It can't be *that* stupid."

"They're convinced that scouts will find out and it'll affect his draft status. That it'd make him a high risk player due to mental instability, forget about Hockey Talks."

"You're right. I take it back. That's the dumbest thing I've heard in my life."

"I know, right?" I rubbed my face. "You can't tell *anyone* that I told you this."

"I won't. I promise."

"Seriously—"

"I said I won't. Jeez. Relax." Heather stepped forward and wrapped her arms around my shoulders. I hugged her back, hands resting on the small of her back. I inhaled her hair. Coconut. She always smelled good.

I remembered when I first met her. Dad just enrolled us in Briar Rose's School for Young Professionals because of their hockey program. Even though I was a much better student than him, Robbie got the full ride and I only got a three-quarter scholarship. It was fall, freshman year, and Heather had just been cast as Red Riding Hood's understudy in a large, regional production of *Into the Woods*. Our school pulled some strings and, for a field trip, took a trek out to see her perform. From the second she stepped onstage, I was hooked. Hooked enough to grow a pair, walk up to her locker the next day at school, and tell her I thought she was great. We'd been nearly inseparable ever since.

When I started to squeeze her more tightly, she pushed me back. "You're playing this weekend, right?"

"Unless I'm a scratch."

"Keisha's singing the anthem so we're all going." By we, I knew she meant her theatre friends, people who were slowly becoming my friends, especially since I started taking an acting class with them in January. "You should come to mine afterward. We're all gonna hang."

Over Heather's shoulder, I could see Robbie with his friends, our teammates. He was way more subdued than he used to be. A year ago, he would have pulled someone into a headlock or jumped on someone's back, forcing them to charge down the hallway, sometimes ramming into football players just for the hell of it. I wondered what would happen if Robbie told the team about his attempt. Would they ask him what it was like getting his stomach pumped, or would they tell him it'd get better? Would they even be his friends? A few years ago, a girl tried to kill herself after her old Myspace got flooded with comments about how fat she was, and someone doxed her, ordering 200 pizzas to her house from Dominos. She butchered her wrists. Afterward, she got bullied even more, especially by her closest friends, and finally her parents moved so she could go to a different school.

But Robbie would always be popular. He'd never be harassed like that girl with the old Myspace page. He was the star center on the first line even though he sometimes spent more time in the penalty box than on the ice. Hooking, holding, tripping. Once, he even knocked out some guy's teeth after the guy pulled a slew foot on our now team captain, Beau.

The bell rang for first block.

"Gotta go," Heather said. She quickly gave me another hug. "Don't forget you're coming to mine after the game, okay? You can stay over and help me practice in the morning. I need to work on extensions." She flashed a smile, waved, and jogged down the hall. I didn't get a chance to tell her that the only way I'd be able to go out was if I talked Robbie into coming with me. She wouldn't have understood anyway.

World Civilizations IV was my first class, and the only class I shared with Robbie. Because Mr. Tan arranged the room alphabetically, I sat right behind him.

"Nice to see you've joined us again, Robert," Mr. Tan said.

Robbie stuck his thumbs up. "Glad to be back, too. You know how much it sucks to not be ten feet away from a toilet? I swear, I lost ten pounds. Food poisoning: the new *Weight Watchers*."

Almost everyone in class burst out laughing. Robbie always had that ability to disarm anyone. Even Mr. Tan barely refrained from chuckling.

"Well, I'm glad you're feeling better."

"Thank you for being so concerned about the state of my ass, Mr. Tan. I shall remember your generosity the next time I worship the porcelain throne." And, with a flourish, he reached into his bag, pulled out a bottle of *Pepto Bismal,* and took a chug. "Mmm, deeeeelliiiiish."

The class started howling. Mr. Tan even wiped his eyes as he gripped his desk for support. Only Robbie could talk about taking a dump and have people worship him like it was the coolest thing ever. How could Robbie act like nothing changed? How could he act like his botched suicide attempt meant nothing to him?

As Mr. Tan began lecturing, Robbie reached into the back pocket of his jeans for his iPhone. Over his shoulder, I caught a glimpse of a Snapchat from Dana, a girl who sat in the back of the class, angled to give a generous view down the front of her shirt. I swore I heard Robbie say, "Ugh," before he shoved his cell in his back pocket, shoulders rounding over his work like it was a needless distraction. Maybe, with hockey always on his mind, that's all it was. A nothing instead of something.

4

We shifted our weight from skate to skate while we waited in the tunnel that led from the locker room to the ice. Leading our pack would be Janek, our starting goalie who was brought to our school on full scholarship plus stipend from the Czech Republic, and bringing up the tail was Ray-Ray, our back up. Most high school teams were less formal than ours, but parents got what they paid for. With Briar Rose's obscene tuition, parents expected the best. We had an NHL-size arena that could hold up to two thousand spectators, enormous locker rooms, showers, and fitness lounges. Students sang the national anthem, announced the play-by-play, and picked which songs to blast during stoppage of play. It might have been high school hockey, but we were so good we usually filled every seat.

Robbie tapped everyone on the shin with his stick, proudly wearing the A on his chest. At the start of the season, Dad lost his shit when Robbie wasn't given captaincy; instead, he shared the role of alternate, but Robbie said it was better that Beau got it. He and Coach Benoit told Dad it was to make him look humble to scouts, but I'd overheard them talking once. Robbie begged to not be given the C, and Coach only gave in once Robbie started getting hysterical.

A horn blared. It was time. Lights flashed across the ice as Janek burst through the gate, leading us in a fast lap around half of the arena. We sped after him, torsos ducked as people cheered. We recognized our schoolmates' faces, their flat palms pounding on the glass as we passed. Once their cheering turned to booing, we didn't need to look to know the other team was here. Tonight we were against Neshanic High. They were always a shoe-in for playoffs with some really huge defensemen. Defense won championships, everyone knew that. While our defense was just as good, we needed our offense to out-skate them. We needed Robbie to beat them.

All our teammates who weren't starters slipped off the ice to the bench. I lingered, glancing at Coach who nodded for me to stay on. It was a gimmick having me on the starting line-up, especially when I'd end up playing less than seven minutes a game, but coach thought it might intrigue scouts and give them ideas, like with the Sedin twins.

Overhead, one of the broadcasting kids called, "At left wing, number nine, Raideeeeeen Hollennnnn." I don't remember a time when Raiden and Robbie weren't on the same line. They were a dynamite duo on the ice and best friends off it, earning them the Rail Road Line nickname, which I thought was really dumb. Raiden grinned crookedly at my brother as the announcer said, "At center, number sixteen, Robbbbbbiiiiieee Bettterrrrby!"

The crowd erupted for my brother, crazy enough for us to feel the vibration through our skates. Most of the guys were good, several would be drafted, but Robbie was the one who was signing autographs already. Robbie didn't soak the attention up. Up until a year ago, he used to engage the crowd, showboat a bit. Now, he gazed ahead at the American flag, grin removed from his face, eyes narrowed in concentration, or prayer.

Their cheering didn't die as the seconds passed. I doubt

anyone heard the announcer call me—Tristan Betterby, number forty-eight, at right wing.

I looked at my twin as the announcer moved to our defense—Smitty and Durrell, and finally Janek, who elicited a roar as loud as Robbie's. Janek wouldn't be draft-eligible for another year, but if he were, it'd be a coin toss whether he or Robbie would be drafted first.

"And now," the announcer continued, "to sing our national anthem, let's welcome Keisha Lewis."

I couldn't help but smile. Keisha was a really great singer and one of the few in the theatre program who already committed to the New School as a junior. We had the same circle of friends, and now shared an acting class ever since I grew the balls to enroll in the one that started in January, but we never hung out on our own. Heather was always there.

Keisha wore one of Robbie's spare jerseys. She was tall, but the jersey dwarfed her. The red complemented her dark skin and hair, today styled out and around her head like a halo, but the bulkiness of the jersey combined with her skinny jeans and tall boots made her look like she was wearing a poncho.

She waited for all of us to take our helmets off before she took a breath and began. If I weren't on the ice, I'd be cheering her on as she belted, *"And the rockets red glare,"* the way everyone else in the stands did.

As Keisha finished, there was extra commotion. I turned my head to see the rest of the theatre kids there, whooping and hollering Keisha's name. I couldn't have missed them in warm-ups; they must have come late and wormed their way to the glass. Heather stood in the front next to Craig, one of the best dancers in the theatre program and the leader of the self-dubbed "Gay-Bros." Heather waved at me and mouthed something I couldn't read. Craig pulled his shirt up and pressed his bare chest to the glass. I tried not to laugh as I put my helmet back on, double-checking to make sure the cage was secure before I took my position at Robbie's side. It was time to buckle down.

The referee moved between Robbie and the opposing center. They kept their heads low, coiled, ready to spring.

As soon as the puck dropped, Robbie was on it. He sent the puck back from the face off to Smitty as Durrell rammed one of their forwards into the boards. I was already rushing down the ice. I might not have been the best player on our team, but I was fast as hell.

Smitty fed the puck to Raiden, who tapped it back toward Robbie. Barely two steps, and Robbie sent it back to Raiden. We'd practiced this play hundreds of times. I'd scoot up the outside and slip in, giving it my best slap shot with Robbie there to catch the rebound while Raiden screened the goalie. If the goalie knocked the rebound out, Raiden would do everything he could to shove it in. We had a sixty-one percent success rate.

"Tristan!" Raiden yelled as he passed me the puck.

The puck connected with my stick and I took off toward goal. The crowd got louder the closer I got to the goalie. The sound of cheering and screaming was addictive. Thinking of the game as a performance revved me up.

The goalie made his move, scooting forward out of the crease, glove out. I envisioned the goal, just high of his blocker. Flashing lights, everyone cheering, especially Heather, who afterward might give me a congratulatory kiss. I pulled my stick back for a slap shot.

"TRISTAN! HEADS UP!" my brother screamed.

The hit came so fast, I didn't know what direction it came

from. My feet left the ice and I flipped onto my back, sliding until I slammed into the boards, hard. From the ice, I saw who hit me: a six-foot-three defender named Kris Jones who was just coming off a seven-game suspension. It might as well have been a freight train. A sea of booing washed through the arena. I glanced toward one of the refs before getting up to see if he'd call it—he didn't.

As I scrambled to pick myself up, Robbie scooted between players, puck miraculously in his possession. The goalie moved toward Robbie, challenging him even farther out of the crease than he'd done with me. Just like me, Robbie lifted his stick. Tension weighted the air; everyone sucked in a breath. Robbie toe-dragged a good two feet to the side then flicked the puck up top shelf so fast the goalie couldn't raise his glove.

The goal horn blared. Everyone screamed. Robbie did this little boogie he always did for his goal celly, fists pumping and hips wiggling. I glanced at the scoreboard: not even twenty seconds after the puck dropped, and Robbie already made it 1-0.

My eyes moved to one section of the arena that was sectioned off as an unofficial press box. A lot of scouts were typing away at their laptops, a few on their mobiles. I scanned the crowd. Our parents would be watching somewhere. At least our dad would be watching; Mom would be on her iPhone. I couldn't see either.

We circled Robbie, tapping each other on the helmet and back before Robbie led us to the bench, fist bunched and bumping past the other players.

"Good choice, Robbie," Coach said, rubbing and clapping his shoulders. "Smart move."

I sat on Robbie's other side. Coach looked at me and gestured down toward the end of the forwards. I slid to the end of the bench. I'd be on the fourth line for the rest of the game.

"It's all right, Butter," Coach said once we changed lines. Everyone on the team had at least one nickname. If you were really good, sometimes you had two or three. I wouldn't have minded Butter if it weren't for the reason. When we were freshmen, our then team captain said, "We should call you guys Butter and Margarine."

"What? *Margarine?*" Robbie had asked. "Why the hell am I margarine?"

"Because," he'd said with a grin, "you're *Better Than Butter.*"

As the game progressed, my time on the ice lessened. I was no longer the gimmick; I now was on the fourth line, dumping and chasing the puck, blocking pucks before they could get to our defense, let alone Janek.

When the end buzzer came, earning us a 3-1 victory— Robbie earning a goal and two assists—I exhaled with relief. Thank God it was over. We skated out to Janek, tapping him on the helmet per tradition before going back to the locker room. Even though we weren't supposed to use our cells in the locker room, I texted Heather, *wait for me.*

I slipped my cell back in my bag as I stripped down. Back in middle school, I used to be self-conscious about changing in front of the others. I think all of us were—the dreaded puberty years—but we got over it quickly. After playing, we were all hot and sweaty and had swamp ass and wanted to cool down. No one really looked or made jokes, except to Henry, whom we joked must have been a porn star in another life, and those were mostly in envious admiration, not that anyone would admit it.

"Good game, boys," Coach Benoit said as we filed in and out of the showers, clapping Robbie on the shoulder with a "you're never going to believe who was here to watch you" gesture. He led Robbie off to the side of the locker room. A huge smile crossed my brother's face—it must have been a big name.

When the next shower became available and I walked under the spray, my heart started pounding rapidly. My head swam. I squeezed my eyes shut, hand pressed to the wall to keep me steady, hot water pounding against my forehead.

"You okay?"

I turned to see Robbie standing there, towel wrapped around his waist. The dizziness immediately cleared. I tried to cover up a bit out of habit. You'd think for all the money the school would have, they could have afforded shower curtains on the stalls. "Yeah, just was a little dizzy," I mumbled as I stepped out of the shower.

"From the hit? They should have called it. If I wasn't in position to get a breakaway, I would have beat his face in." Robbie took my place, still keeping the towel on under the spray. I didn't know what that was about, and like hell anyone would ask.

"Sure," I said as I left the room, grabbing a towel and drying off as I moved. I stopped halfway out and turned back to my brother. "I need you to do me a huge favor."

"Hm?" Robbie said, a full foamy lather over his hair.

"Heather invited me to a party."

"So go."

I stared at him, trying to figure out a code word to remind him I had to stay by his side. Robbie looked at me blankly, then groaned as he finally got it. Rinsing the lather, he said, "We're all supposed to go to Durrell's though."

"What's this about?" Durrell asked, stepping out of the next shower. At six-foot-two, Durrell was a menacing stay-at-home defenseman, crushing our opponents into the boards. One of those guys who was great at everything. He always made honor roll, and he'd be drafted when he was eligible next year, barely missing the high school window with a March birthday while Robbie and I made it on the last day of deadline in September. Durrell did golf and ran track in the off-season. He played guitar in a band and was even the secretary of the Political Science club. He was already offered a full ride to every college he applied to, hell, probably even from colleges he *didn't* apply to. All the girls had crushes on him. Literally. Except the lesbians, and even then they thought he was awesome.

Because really, he was *that* cool.

"Heather's having some people over," I said. "Was trying to see if Robbie would go with me."

"Can anyone go?" Durrell asked.

I blinked a few times. "I uh. . . I don't know. I guess a few?"

"I'm down," Durrell said suddenly.

". . . you are?"

"Yeah. Solidarity with Robbie."

"What about solidarity with Robbie?" Raiden asked, walking into an adjacent shower. That was the one crappy thing about a team; there were never secrets.

"We're going to Heather's instead of mine to party," Durrell said.

Raiden looked confused. Or maybe he was just squinting under the showerhead's heavy spray. "Who the hell's Heather?"

"She's that girl who Tristan hangs out with all the time," Robbie said. "You know, the one who's in all of the musicals?"

"She hot?"

"Not my type," Robbie mumbled.

"Then nope. I don't know her."

"Hey," Janek called, Czech accent heavier the way it always

was after the physical exertion of a game. Like it sucked out his energy to force an American accent. "So we're partying at Heather's now?"

"I don't know if this is a great idea," I said hurriedly. "I don't want to just, like, invite the whole team without asking her."

"So ask her," Durrell said. "We'll contribute pizza money and beer."

"And wings. Can't go without wings," Beau added as he slipped into another shower stall. "Did I forget anything?"

"Chips," Janek said. "And guacamole. And what are they called? The things that look like M&Ms?"

"Reese's Pieces or Skittles?" Beau asked.

"Both," Janek said. "Definitely both."

Robbie gave me the corniest thumbs up he could muster, like he was saying, *Hey, you got your way,* even though he damn well knew I didn't.

I hurried to change into a clean pair of underwear, nice jeans, and a dark, long-sleeved polo shirt. Tucked to the side was a spare change of clothes and board shorts, the things I always brought to Heather's enormous house with its hot tub. Throwing my bag over my shoulder, I wove through the corridors until I got on the main concourse. The second Heather's friends saw me—a group of about fifteen—they started cheering. I ducked my head, embarrassed.

When I was close enough, I said, "Great job, Keisha."

Heather cut Keisha off before she could speak, "I think you stole the show with your gymnastic prowess."

"Gymnastics? I thought it was a touchdown," Craig added.

I groaned. "Please don't tell me it was that obvious?"

"Back of your jersey said T. BETTERBY." Heather nudged me playfully. "You ready?"

"Uh, yeah. So about that," I began slowly, clearing my throat. "I kind of messed up."

"What do you mean?" Heather's eyes became harsh.

"I asked Robbie about coming, and Durrell heard, and Durrell thought it was an open invite so . . ." I shifted my weight and mumbled, "I think a bunch of the guys want to come over . . . like all of them."

"Are you serious?" Heather gawked.

"They said they'd pay for pizza and beer and whatever," I said hurriedly. "They'd hold good on that. I mean, I could tell them to get lost, but uh . . ."

Craig lifted his arms to the side like a cross and gazed at the ceiling. "OH, LAWDY, THANK YOU JAAAAYYYZUSSS!"

"Huh?"

Craig simply beamed. "You're telling me a bunch of gorgeous, ripped hockey studs are coming to Heather's humble abode?"

"Gorgeous?" I snorted. "Most of them don't have teeth."

Craig seemed to think for a moment. "I can live with dentures."

"Enough about dentures." Heather beamed, though something didn't quite seem sincere. "If they're willing to pay for beer and pizza, I'm okay with it."

I rubbed the back of my neck. "So, uh, I guess I'll meet you guys there?"

"Absolutely. We need to get ready," Heather said, wrapping an arm around Craig's back and the other around Keisha's shoulder. "Come on, dolls."

Keisha looked over her shoulder at me and smiled. I half-waved, then hustled back to the locker room. The guys were already laughing about the party and how wild it'd be with all the theatre girls. Some were making bets on how many girls they'd make out with, and what about making out with two at a time? These bets were broken up with claps on my back, the guys telling me how awesome I was for organizing this.

Except it wasn't awesome. At all. In fact, it kind of sucked.

"You ready to go?" Robbie asked by Raiden's side.

No, I thought as I led them out of the locker room and into the frigid night.

5

Parties at Heather's house had always been fun. Her mom worked graveyard shifts so nothing was off-limits: the pool, the hot tub, even the spare bedroom. The few times her mom got a night off, she sometimes joined us, jokingly asking which of the guys were straight and over eighteen. Awkward.

Almost as awkward as the way the team walked in, standing with their thumbs hooked in their pockets around the island in the kitchen, drinking beer that Beau got with his fake ID. Usually once I got to Heather's, she'd turn on the hot tub, everyone would get in our bathing suits, and jump in. Sometimes there'd be a few make-outs, or tops might come off from quasi-drunken dares. But my teammates didn't have bathing suits, so no way that was going to happen even though Craig slipped out and turned the jets on. Wishful thinking, I guess.

I stood near the sliding glass door, watching steam rise from the hot tub. Small snowflakes dropped from the sky; it was pretty.

Heather handed me a bottle of Smirnoff Ice Raspberry Burst. I didn't like beer, but malt tasted pretty close to soda. Especially the Raspberry kind. Grape was just vile. I opened the top and took a sip as Heather filled a cooler with other bottles.

"What's with the pussy drink?" Ray-Ray asked, sipping

from a can of Moosehead. Because, really, what else would a bunch of hockey players drink?

"It's just . . . something we do," I mumbled, torn between putting the drink down or downing it fast. But, to my surprise, Durrell moved in.

"Mind if I give it a try?" he asked Heather. Smooth.

She grinned as she opened a bottle and handed it over. "It's cheesy, but I really do like it."

"I can see why." He grinned and she laughed. I looked around the kitchen—my brother wasn't in here. So much for Durrell coming in solidarity with my brother.

Music started blasting. I recognized the song as Garrix's "Animals," which we always played in warm-ups to get us pumped. Heather's face gave the faintest twitch, but she said nothing.

There was commotion in the next room. I ducked my head in. A bunch of the guys sat around her 65" TV playing a copy of NHL 16 that Smitty always kept in his bag on Heather's XBox. A few of the acting kids crowded around them, Ray-Ray already making out with a girl I barely knew named Tina, while Beau's girlfriend—he must have picked her up on the way over—rubbed his shoulders as he played against Janek.

My brother was on the couch next to Raiden, chucking Doritos at Janek's head any time he made a mistake in the game.

"That's what you get for playing as the Rangers!" Robbie taunted, breaking into laughter when Janek turned his head, catching a chip in his mouth.

"Hugh five!" Raiden said to Robbie as they slapped their hands. I'm not sure why they started saying Hugh Five instead of High Five, but it stuck enough for everyone in the locker room to pick it up, even Coach Benoit. I thought it was kind of stupid, but I thought almost anything my brother came up with was stupid. Especially if it was something my brother came up *with* Raiden. Then it was extra stupid.

"Hey, T," Durrell said as he walked next to me, bottle of Amstel Light in his hand. Talk about being pretty quick to ditch the Smirnoff Ice.

"Hey. Where'd Heather go?"

"She went to change into a bathing suit. Something about a hot tub." Durrell leaned against the counter. "You want to join us?"

"Do you even have a bathing suit?" I asked skeptically.

"Underwear's close enough. Figure that's enough to stay modest, not that I care." I hesitated enough for Durrell to pick up on it. "Hey, I know you two are kinda tight. You okay with this?"

"With what?"

"With me getting to know Heather. She's really cool."

I wanted to say no. I really did. Instead, I said, "Hot tub sounds great. Give me a few to change."

"Cool. We'll save you a spot, T."

"Great," I muttered, trying to sound enthusiastic as I walked up the steps to Heather's room where I stashed my hockey bag. I rifled through it for my board shorts and changed into them, deciding whether I was going to ditch my shirt or not. I pulled it off and looked in the mirror. Not bad. Not that Heather ever noticed.

When I stepped into the hallway, I almost collided with my brother and Raiden.

"What are you doing up here?" Robbie asked, eyebrow raising.

"Could ask you the same thing," I retorted, noticing the

pipe in Raiden's hand. "You can't just smoke up in Heather's house."

"We're not going to smoke up," Raiden said with a buzzed slur, arm draped around Robbie's shoulder. "We're totally going to watch *Lifetime* movies and cuddle."

"Totally," Robbie said, unable to keep a straight face as he nudged Raiden with his hip. "Because Raid's all about having a good cry."

"Totally good cry."

They moved around me, peering into rooms before turning into the guest room. They closed the door behind them. There was the loud click of the lock.

So much for not smoking up.

I walked down the steps and out the sliding door, shivering in the frigid air. True to his word, there was a space for me between Durrell and Keisha; Heather sat on Durrell's other side, Craig next to her.

"Oh, thank GOD you're here," Craig said, snorting. "There was a severe lack of penis."

Next to me, Durrell stiffened. I looked at Craig, gesturing for him to cut it out. He ignored me. "Seriously, I haven't gotten some in like . . . two weeks."

"A new record. You must be proud," Heather taunted.

"You're acting like that's a bad thing," Craig said, voice rising in a sing-song.

"It kind of is," Durrell said, pulling a face. "Seriously, don't you have any self-respect?"

"Like the hockey guys aren't hooking up whenever they can?" Craig brushed him off. "I'm pretty sure Raymond's shoving his tongue down as many girls' throats as he can."

"That's because Ray-Ray's an idiot," Durrell reasoned. When Craig groaned, Durrell continued, "No, seriously. He's really stupid. The bulk of us aren't, though. I mean, Tristan's got his head on straight."

"Don't," I cut in sharply. Last thing I needed was Heather to go off in a peel about me still having my V-card.

Durrell nodded, picking up on it, changing the topic, "Beau's always got a steady girlfriend. No one's really flaunting anything, you know?"

"What exactly do you mean by 'flaunting'?" Craig asked.

"Well . . . you know."

Craig's eyes narrowed. "Actually, I don't. How about you elaborate?"

"You're going to twist my words and try to make me sound homophobic."

"I don't think I need to twist your words. I think I read you loud and clear." Craig stood up with a tight-lipped smile and got out of the hot tub. "I think I've overstayed my welcome." He hurried back into the house. I wasn't sure whether I should follow him or stay with Heather and Durrell and the others.

Keisha shot Durrell an angry look. "I dare you to tell any of your teammates that they should have integrity." Then she climbed out of the hot tub and hustled into the house after Craig.

"Ignore them," Heather said, turning to face Durrell. "They're drama queens."

"Craig looked really hurt," I said loudly. But Heather ignored me as she brushed a wet strand of hair out of her eyes. I cleared my throat. "We should check on him."

"You do that," she said, not even looking at me.

"I said we."

"I know."

I hesitated before climbing out of the hot tub and into her

house, for a moment tempted to turn the lock on the sliding door when Durrell put his arm around Heather's shoulder.

I walked through the house, but most of the theatre kids had left. Peering out the front door, I couldn't see Craig's car. I couldn't blame them. Leaving sounded like a great idea. I walked up the steps and down the hall to Heather's room. After changing in my regular clothes, I went to the guest room then knocked on the door. "Hey, Robbie? You still in there?"

There was a scuffling before the door unlocked and Robbie poked his head out. Surprisingly, he didn't smell like weed. "What?"

"Let's go."

"Are you serious? We just got here."

"Yeah, but this party sucks."

"I already was nice enough to come here instead of Durrell's."

"But—"

"I'll get you when I'm ready. Jesus Christ, can't you just fuck off for a while?"

And, with that, Robbie slammed the door in my face.

I stood outside the door for several minutes before I trudged down the steps with my hockey bag, curling up on one of Heather's chairs, listening to the guys holler over NHL 16 until I fell asleep.

6

It was hard to write or concentrate on anything with Robbie close enough for our breath to sometimes synchronize. I opened a Word doc, fingers hovering above my keyboard. It had been a while since I'd written anything, but I usually got the itch whenever shit hit the fan, or when I was annoyed with Robbie. I gazed at the screen and typed:

There were creatures that lived in caves on the beach. Their skin was slick and gray like dolphins, even though they had legs and couldn't swim.

I tried to continue, but Robbie's presence grew, distracting me, getting closer, like the table was shrinking. My room was no longer my room. Even Robbie's smell was stronger than mine, invading the air. His stuff pushed into mine, bigger and messier. His problems were bigger and messier too. The silent suicide attempt clung like a leech on my right to brood and figure out my own shit.

The bunk bed took up almost the whole wall, covering my few posters. While Robbie had hockey posters, mostly of the different players on the New Jersey Devils, I had two prints of abstract paintings and one poster of Patina Miller that Heather gave me for my eighteenth birthday. Only now that it was gone did I realize I needed one space to exist independently of him.

Forcing myself to stare at my computer screen, I tried to

continue. There now was a smaller house of the dolphin people, all little orphans who had to be the adults in their little hut, lying horizontally on their beds so all of them would fit. They rotated positions because the littlest dolphin person who slept on the bed wet himself whenever he had nightmares, which was almost nightly.

"What are you writing?"

Robbie leaned to the side, trying to peer at my computer. His headphones hung around his neck, Tori Amos's voice now distinguishable through the speakers.

"Stuff," I answered curtly, index finger hovering over the mouse, wondering if I should minimize the window.

"Can I see?"

"There's nothing to see."

"Looks like something."

I started to type again. I only made it through half a paragraph with Robbie's gaze on me. He was hesitating, like he wanted to say something but was figuring out how to make it not sound stupid. I let him struggle a bit longer. Having the upper hand, even for just a few minutes, was small revenge, but I'd take it.

Finally, Robbie said, "Remember last year in English when we all had to write short stories?"

Of course I remembered. The teachers saved creative writing for the end of the year when everyone was lethargic and reading books seemed unbearable. It made the month on Charles Dickens's *Great Expectations* more bearable. "Yeah, why?"

"Do you still have that story you wrote? The one that was like *Inception* meets *Being John Malkovich*?"

Red warning lights went off in my head. Robbie didn't do nice, and he didn't do nostalgic either. Even if he changed over the past year, he couldn't have changed *that* much. This had to be a set up, but I wasn't sure for what. And that scared the hell out of me.

See, "Trapped in Stardust" was a short story I wrote last year. It was about two juniors, Jeremy and Melissa, who are best friends. Jeremy is in love with Melissa, but she's in love with a superhero named Stardust. Jeremy decides that the only way to get Melissa's attention is to kill Stardust, but he accidentally gets sucked into Stardust's body. He thinks it's pretty cool at first since he gets to make out with Melissa a lot, but then, realizing he can't control Stardust's body, comes to loathe being intimate with Melissa while she loved somebody else. I got a B+ on it because our teacher Miss Maroney, who self-published a paranormal romance trilogy about a stripper and a figure-skating werewolf—I shit you not—said Melissa should have realized that it was Jeremy at the end and fallen in love with him, breaking the spell that got him trapped in Stardust's body.

But it wasn't like that in real life. Best friends never fell in love. Couples who were best friends only became best friends *after* they got together.

Robbie asked, "Can you email it to me? I want to read it again."

"Why?"

"Because it was good."

"Not good enough for an A," I muttered.

"Because Miss Maroney's a stupid bitch," Robbie snorted. I forgot he had bad turf with her as well. When we got our short story assignment, for once Robbie seemed excited about doing his homework. So excited that he actually would knock on my door to ask me about plot devices and generic grammar. He actually thanked me. When Robbie's name was called, he got to his feet, story in hand, and cleared his throat. In a horrible English accent, he said, "Good evening, ladies and gentlemen. My name is Robert Betterby and I'd like to present my story, 'Michael Bay is a Douchebag.'" I could barely hear Robbie's voice over the other students' laughter. In his story, Quentin Tarantino and Martin Scorsese are the bosses of the notorious director mafia. To save the IQs of future generations, Tarantino and Scorsese decide that they need to burn Michael Bay's scripts and hire Matt Stone and Trey Parker as their hit men. It featured Optimus Prime, Captain America, an appearance from Rainbow Dash, a voiceover by James Earl Jones, and the accidental death of Tarantino and Scorsese by "*divine intervention*"—in this case, Matt Stone and Trey Parker's lethal farts (no, really). It ended with Michael Bay announcing that he'd be doing a remake of *Fried Green Tomatoes*—now enhanced with *EXPLOSIONS!* BOOM-O!

Robbie got a standing ovation, a "see me after class," and four days of detention after he told Miss Maroney that she wasn't qualified to critique him if she couldn't get a traditional publisher to pick up her shitty figure skating werewolf trilogy.

But that was last year when Robbie was loud and reeked confidence. When he tormented anyone who stood in his path. Before he thought wearing a fake lip piercing was cool, became mostly silent, and overdosed on leftover Percocet.

"Are you going to take her advice? Make it the happy love story?" Robbie asked, pushing the silver ball on his fake lip ring around until it clicked against his teeth.

"No. Best friends don't get together in real life."

"Like you and Heather?"

Without answering, I turned back to the computer, biting back a scowl. I knew there was a catch. Robbie wasn't interested in my writing; he was just looking for another chance to rip on me. With enough ammunition, it'd spread around the locker room, spill into the halls.

"I'm right, aren't I?" Robbie said with glee. "That it was about you two?"

I reached for my headphones. Three years ago, Heather and I were acting out a scene when she said, "There's this thing I learned in acting class today. A fake kiss. Just put your hand up in front of your mouth." We only did it once. I kind of wanted to do it again, without hands, but didn't ask. She never brought it up again.

Only a few minutes passed before Robbie tapped me on the shoulder *again*. I took off my headphones. "What?"

"Is it harder to write fan-fiction or original fiction?"

"Excuse me?" I questioned, enunciating my words slowly although my heart rate slightly quickened. How did Robbie even know what fanfic was? This was bad. Really bad. I sometimes wrote stories with Heather when we were chatting on Skype and her voice teacher wanted to give her a rest. Well, really, it started as roleplaying—her typing a paragraph and me responding as another character, then Heather asking me to edit it into a story for her, upping the drama and tension and sometimes sex.

Robbie couldn't know about that, could he?

"Is it easier to write your stuff on your own, or the fanfic stuff with Heather?"

He turned his computer screen toward me. Indeed it was there, an account that Heather created on Archive of Our Own where she posted our stories. There wasn't much. Just a little something here and there about *Doctor Who* or *Sherlock* or whatever Heather's current obsession was that she got me hooked on. I pictured my twin's old personality telling everybody at school at lunchtime, goading everyone to join in, being pegged with Heather as losers. Although probably people would let Heather be; Heather was a girl, and girls were allowed to write fanfic, especially when they had promising acting careers. But guys? Yeah, right. Especially if those guys played hockey, even reluctantly.

Cautiously, I asked, "How'd you know about that?"

"A year or two ago, Heather was talking about something on Facebook she was writing with 'a friend.' Linked up her site and saw stuff was written by GlitterB0mb and Silenced1. Kind of figured that was you. I looked at your profile and stories. The ones you write on your own are way better. I've been meaning to bring it up for a while but kept forgetting."

I didn't know what sort of excuse I could use to keep Robbie from teasing me. He'd rip on me no matter what the fandom was. "Don't tell anyone," I said, mind racing to think of what I had to bribe him.

Robbie's brow raised. "Why wouldn't I? It's good."

What?

"Seriously I wish I could write like half as good as you. Your Batman thing was fucking awesome."

"Stop messing with me."

"I'm not," Robbie said. "Seriously, the guys would go nuts over this. It's really freaking good." His eyes lowered and he fidgeted with his headphones. "You're lucky you're smart enough to do college. If I don't get drafted, I'm screwed."

"You're gonna be in Juniors once you commit to a team. And you're *definitely* getting drafted."

"But I wasn't drafted to a Junior team," Robbie protested.

"Neither was I."

Robbie bit his lip and put his headphones back on. Like he wasn't sure whether I insulted him.

I turned to my screen, though I kept glancing at my twin,

who now was watching hockey fights on Youtube. The profile of his shadow took up half of the wall, making the room feel even tinier. I didn't trust any compliment that came out of his mouth, although these few were different. He'd never mentioned any interest in college hockey before. Not that I could remember. And he never acknowledged me being smart. Maybe he was just trying to make our living situation less awkward now that I was pretty much his babysitter. I'd never be able to figure Robbie out. I wasn't even sure I wanted to. Sometimes people just weren't meant to be close. We fell under that category, and I kept trying to believe that I was okay with it.

Spoiler alert: I wasn't.

7

One of the things I loved best about acting class was that we always started at barre. A few of the "serious students" (aka the jerkoffs who thought musicals were a lesser art) complained, only wanting to perform in plays or on screen, but our teacher Ms. Price insisted that we needed to be well-rounded. She pointed out the choreography in stage plays such as *The Curious Incident of the Dog in the Night-Time* where the protagonist Christopher, a fifteen-year-old with autism, went through scene-by-scene doing impressive, gravity defying moves, getting flipped in the air by the company or walking across the walls. It was hard for the "serious students" to argue with such an award-winning play.

Doing warm ups in a class instead of with a Youtube video was invigorating. I always warmed up behind Craig. He was the best male dancer at Briar Rose and did cheer in fall. He always said his body craved ballet and it was almost physically painful to take a day off. I could believe it as I watched him, mimicking his movement as best as I could. Even though Heather taught me a lot, there were some limitations learning from someone with different anatomy than mine.

Convincing my parents I knew what I was doing when I registered for this acting class—more than halfway through our season and just after the new year—wasn't easy. I'd lied my way through by saying they were easy electives to get As. Mom especially hated anything related to theatre. I think it made her sad. On the living room mantel was a picture of our Uncle Anthony framed in white gold. He died during a run of *Smokey Joe's Cafe*. Cancer, she told us with glossy, hurt eyes. Apparently, he didn't even tell Mom he was sick.

The exciting thing was that with each class, Ms. Price corrected my position less and less, complimenting me on my learning curve as she pushed me for just a bit more, a few straighter lines, putting her hand on the back of my calf as I raised it as high as I could, moving it away when my foot was head level. Only two weeks later, and I could do that on my own without assistance, and without holding the barre for support.

"You've really never had acting classes before?" Ms. Price asked skeptically, arms folded across her chest. *I wish*, I wanted to say, but I didn't.

"Just these few weeks with you, but Heather's taught me a lot," I said as I lowered my leg. Across the room, Heather beamed at me. "She's awesome."

"Yes, she's very good, but no formal training? From a professional?"

Heather's smile faded just a hair. I rubbed the back of my neck. "Um. Youtube?"

"Amazing," Ms. Price said, shaking her head in admiration. "Absolutely amazing. I wish I had you when you were a kid. You'd be on Broadway by now."

My breath caught. I had to look at the floor. "That's an exaggeration."

"No. That's an understatement." She smiled at me. "You really should audition for the spring musical. We're doing *The Drowsy Chaperone*."

"But hockey . . ."

"Doesn't your season end in March if you make playoffs? February if you don't?" Ms. Price grinned. "See? I do my homework."

I felt a strange warmth in my eyes, like I could cry. "You . . . really want me to audition?"

"I *need* you to." Ms. Price pressed her hands on my shoulders. I had to take a slow, shaky breath as I met her eyes. Until a couple of weeks ago, Ms. Price only knew me from sometimes helping Heather out backstage with her makeup, an unofficial dresser. Now, she wanted me to audition? "Take a breather," she said, giving a squeeze as if she could read my whirring mind. "Five minutes, okay?"

Mutely, I nodded and hopped in a seat a little way from the group as Ms. Price began discussing monologues and the order we'd do them in, whether we'd be singing if we were concentrating on musical theatre or doing something from a play.

I pressed the heels of my palms to my eyes and inhaled slowly. Ms. Price didn't hand out compliments on a plate. I wasn't sure what was more overwhelming: the fact I had the potential to be on a Broadway stage or that she actually saw something in me. Anger mixed in with that blissful revelation. If I didn't play hockey, I could have had a chance. My parents knew since I was eight that I wouldn't be the player Robbie was. I could have started acting younger. I could have been a star, just like Robbie. They kept that from me.

"You okay, Tristan?" Heather asked, sitting next to me.

"Sort of. Just a bit overwhelmed."

"I'm glad I was able to help you get noticed by Ms. Price," she said with a smile. Then, she quickly added, "I asked her if we could do something together instead of monologues. She said to ask you about it. So, what do you say to a duet?"

"That sounds great, but I kind of prepared something."

"Oh. Well, if you don't want to . . ."

"It's not that I don't want to," I said hurriedly. "I just wanted to give something a try. A test run in case I go on with the audition."

"Yeah. Okay."

"Maybe next time?"

"Maybe next time I'll want to do a duet with Craig," Heather said.

I sighed. Heather could be impossible if she had an idea and it didn't go to plan. Plus, she had great taste. "So, what'd you have in mind?"

"Well," she said, eyes lighting up as she dug through her bag and handed me a copy of "Inside Out" from *A Gentleman's Guide to Love and Murder*.

"Okay," I said, nodding more eagerly. My solo plans could wait a class—doing a romantic duet with Heather would be a bonus, even though Monty's part was kind of small in that song

"Great!" she chirped as she sat next to me with her own sheet music, tapping on my thigh with her index finger as she silently mouthed the words. My eyes were glued to her fingers. In the background, Keisha started singing "Losing My Mind" from *Follies* but I couldn't process her voice.

Heather's fingers danced higher up my thigh. "If we kill it, I'll bring you with me to a show this weekend," she whispered.

"Okay," I whispered back, even though I wasn't sure how I could convince my parents to let me go. But that didn't matter. Not when we were going to go onstage, sheet music in hand, Ms. Price on the piano, and kill it. And, when it was finally our turn, belting and looking into each other's eyes, voices clear and passionate, that's exactly what we did. Killed it enough for a standing ovation and for Heather to throw her arms around my shoulders, letting me lift and twirl her before the bell rang. In the corner of my eye, I saw Keisha give the saddest smile I've ever seen before she got her purse and backpack and walked out.

"You were divine," Heather whispered, fingers linking with mine. "You made me sound amazing."

"You were perfect," I replied as I squeezed her hand, smiling as we walked together until we split ways for our next class. Maybe it was a matter of time before she'd suggest we change our Facebook statuses. Maybe it was a matter of time before she'd let me kiss her for real. Maybe it'd happen this weekend once I convinced my parents to let me go see a show with her instead of staying home with Robbie.

Maybe this would be it. Erase Durrell's arm around Heather's shoulder in the hot tub and replace it with mine. Think about our sides pressed together, Heather running her hands over years of hardened muscle. Like the time I once thought something would happen when Heather had a party over the summer, and I took off my shirt, and the girls kept wanting to feel my abs. Or like the time I thought something would happen when Heather rose her leg in arabesque and asked me to lift her and was so strong in her poise, it felt like she literally weighed nothing before she twisted her body over my shoulder, arms above her head, crotch too close to my face for me not to wonder if it was intentional and did anyone notice my hard on.

Maybe this was it.

8

"All right, boys!" Coach Benoit said after setting up cones, dividing the ring in two. "We're finishing off the long weekend with some speed. You don't need to go one hundred percent fast one hundred percent of the time, but for this, you do. Anyone who isn't on the verge of puking when they're done will have to go again and again until they're vomiting blood. Understood?"

Even though all the guys groaned, I couldn't help but grin. Gameless weekends were the *best*. Especially the gameless weekends when Coach told us to take time off. He was always conservative when it came to preventing injury; it wasn't worth wrecking some of the main prospects, i.e. Robbie.

Any break from hockey was nice, but this particular break corresponded with the miracle of Mom agreeing to watch Robbie so I could go into the city with Heather and see a show, her treat. In fact, they even said I could stay there for the weekend, like it was some sort of prize for good behavior. I was pretty sure the real reason was that they had made plans with Robbie, probably involving scouting, or a road trip to see the Devils take on the Sabres up in Buffalo.

That didn't matter. They could do whatever the hell they wanted to if that meant going to Heather's for the weekend and seeing a mysterious show, aka she hadn't bought the tickets yet and would text me her decision.

This was probably the best practice of my life, even though I couldn't wait for it to be over. Yesterday's practice ended up with one-timers, today we'd be racing. I made it halfway through the one-timers yesterday before I got out. Durrell beat Robbie at the very end, at which point Robbie over-dramatically dropped his stick to the ice, pressed his hands to his face, and belted out, "WHYYYYY, GOD? WHYYYYYY???? *AY DIO MIOOOOOOO!*"

"All right, boys!" Coach yelled as he divided us in teams of two, starting with the goalies, then the defenders, and finally the forwards. When Robbie and Raiden started jawing each other, Coach shook his head. "Not today, boys. Margarine versus Butter."

Immediately, I cringed. Admittedly, I was damn fast, and definitely had won my fair share of matches, but pitting me up against Robbie was just cruel. Especially when Raiden snickered, "Already know that outcome."

"Knock it off," Robbie said, shoving him. "He's fast."

"But you're faster."

Coach blew his whistle, instructing us to get set. I watched Janek and Ray-Ray line up, crouched forward with their sticks and heavy goalie pads. When Coach blew his whistle and they were off, we couldn't keep from laughing and cheering. There was always something hilarious about goalies whenever they raced, or fought, or did anything "fast." Especially when those goalies were Janek and Ray-Ray. Maybe from all the pucks they take to the head, or the absolute joy they had in taking off, skidding wildly around the ends of the ring. Ray-Ray hustled to pull ahead of Janek, skating backwards for the last few steps as he gestured toward his crotch and yelled, "Suck it!"

Coach blew the whistle again, not giving anyone time to celebrate as our next duo took off—Durrell against Smitty—then the next and the next. Robbie and I were dead last. As the pair before us moved out and we took our spots, I glanced at my twin. We had an identical stance. I crouched forward, toe digging into the ice. If I wasn't prepared to spring, I wouldn't stand a chance.

The second the whistle came, we were flying. We pumped our arms for more momentum as our legs shoved off in fast, hard skates. Our bodies fell in near perfect alignment. Our teammates screamed and I pressed on, ignoring the sting in my lungs as I leaned into the corner, sliding fast on the last stretch back as everyone cheered wildly. My heart pounded faster than from adrenaline alone. Robbie wasn't in my line of sight.

As I skated hard, maybe eleven strides from the finish, I saw it. A flash of jersey fabric. Robbie came out of nowhere, charging on the end rush. I kept my head low, my lungs burning as I stretched out, elongating my body, and crossed the finish line a step-and-a-half before Robbie. I doubled over, hands pressed to my thighs as I tried to catch my breath, grinning ear to ear.

"Damn it!" Robbie swore, slamming down his stick hard enough for it to snap.

My grin disappeared. I shrank back until Coach Benoit said, "Good job, Butter."

"Man, if I were a fraction as fast as you," Beau said, shaking his head with rare admiration. A compliment from the team captain always felt good, even if it came at Robbie's expense.

"All right, boys. We're done. Have a good weekend, and don't do anything stupid. I'm looking at you, Ray-Ray," Coach said, clapping his hands. But, before we could move, he added, "Margarine, stay here."

I glanced at my brother, who hung his head. Raiden tapped Robbie's shin with his stick as he passed, a sympathetic frown on his face. As I skated to the tunnel, I heard Coach's voice. "You skated like shit."

"I tried, Coach."

Queasiness settled in my stomach. I knew I shouldn't have been listening, but I stalled in the tunnel.

Coach's tone became harsher. "No room for trying. Only doing."

"I thought I did."

"You want to be drafted? You want to be the best forward on the team?"

"It was one stupid exercise. It wasn't like it was a game."

"You want that stupid exercise to give your competition ammunition?"

"Ray-Ray freaking *moonwalked* over the finish."

"Ray-Ray's an idiot. What if a scout was watching? You need to be one hundred percent all the time. No time to be some weak-ass pansy. Give in a little, and they'll make you bend over and take it. Understood?"

Robbie shrunk. "Yes, Coach."

"What aren't you going to do?"

"Bend over and take it."

"Again. Louder."

My brother's voice became terse. "I'm not going to bend over and take it."

Coach Benoit nodded. "Forty laps as fast as possible. Then you can shower up. Maybe next time you'll actually win."

I hustled into the locker room so they wouldn't know I was

listening. I changed and scooted off into the shower. Most of the guys had already left practice. By the time I came out, Robbie was sitting on the bench with his head in his hands. He was fully dressed, except for his helmet. His body was drenched in sweat, hair flat against his scalp. Robbie's shoulders curled in. I smoothed out my polo shirt and sat next to him on the bench. "What's wrong?"

Robbie got to his feet. He pulled off his jersey. "Let's go home."

"Is Coach still pissed that I beat you?"

"Really, Tristan? *Really?*"

I shut up. Fine. It didn't matter. If he didn't want an ounce of empathy, I wouldn't give it to him.

So, why was that getting harder to accept?

We left the locker room and headed out to the parking lot. Snow dusted the sidewalk. As I got into the driver's side, my phone buzzed with a text message from Heather. One acronym: *POTO.*

9

The best thing about living in North Jersey was that we could hop on any bus or train straight to New York Penn Station. We mostly walked around Times Square and the theatre district, coughing in the smog and hanging out by the stage door after the show for autographs. The last time we went into the city, we saw *Wicked.* That was Heather's favorite musical. It was kind of growing on me even though at first I thought it was overrated. The time before, we saw *Rock of Ages,* which had kick-ass, old rock songs from the eighties. The time before that, we saw *Matilda,* which I said was only okay even though I loved it. Heather caught my bluff because she suggested we do Trunchbull and Miss Honey for Halloween at her party. Instead I went as Gabe from *Next to Normal* and wore just my underwear. Everyone was all over me, except Heather, so it was almost great.

I packed a toiletry bag and finished my hair, wondering how close to the chandelier we'd be able to sit, whether we'd get first cast or understudies, what sort of effects would be used.

On a hanger were my dress pants, a pressed white shirt, and a slim, burgundy tie. On another hanger, I had a navy sports jacket. I figured I could decide how dressy I should be at that last minute.

A loud crash came from downstairs, followed by shouting.

I dropped my backpack and clothes before taking off down the steps. "Everything okay?"

Robbie stood in the kitchen looking wild. He gripped a kitchen knife. With his back against the sink, he rotated his arm, pointing it back and forth between Mom and Dad. "I can't do it," Robbie spluttered hysterically. "Don't make me. Please don't make me do it."

"Robbie, put it down," Dad said, trying to inch forward. "Put it down."

"Stay back!" he yelled.

Mom gripped her iPhone with her red fingernails. "Should I call 911?"

"Yes," I said at the same time Dad said, "No. We've got this."

My throat tightened. Did he really think it'd be better to risk getting stabbed than Robbie getting some help? I wanted to argue with Dad, to yell at him, but I couldn't. He wouldn't listen to me.

I inched closer. "Hey, Robbie? Look at me."

I caught my brother's eyes. They didn't look right. He didn't look like some crazed madman, or some psychopath. He looked . . . scared.

"Come on," I said. "Put it down. You're freaking me out."

Robbie held the knife at me then dropped his eyes to his wrist. It was like I could hear him in my head. *It'd be so easy . . .*

"Don't," I said firmly, stepping closer. "Put it down."

He whimpered.

"Put it down. Now."

Robbie's shaking hand dropped the knife to the floor. He covered his face, doubling over as he sobbed. I scooted forward and kicked the knife across the kitchen. Then I gripped Robbie's shoulders.

"Shh. It's okay."

"I can't do it," he gasped.

"That's a good thing. You don't want to cut anyone—"

"No! I *can't* do it. You're not listening! No one fucking listens!" Robbie's knees buckled. By instinct, I wrapped my arms around his waist, keeping him from hitting the floor. I glanced at my parents, both white as sheets and mute. I guess my silence was inherited if none of us could communicate.

I walked Robbie to the steps, helping him up one step at a time until we got to my room. I guided him to my lower bunk. He dropped heavily on it before curling on his side, shaking.

"I can't do it. I can't. I can't."

"Shh. It's okay."

"You know I want to, right?" he asked, desperately.

"Want to what?"

My brother couldn't answer. I sighed, untied his sneakers, and pulled them off along with his socks, damp from sweat. He still hadn't showered. His shaking body slowed when I pulled my blanket over him. With a sigh, I got out my cellphone and dialed up Heather.

"Hey, Tristan," she greeted.

My chest ached. "I can't go."

There was a long pause on the line. "Are you serious?"

"I'm sorry—"

"I got you a ticket to *Phantom* and you can't go."

"It's Robbie," I said, keeping my voice low.

"What about him?"

I looked at the lump on the lower bunk. "I'll explain later. In person."

"Unbelievable," Heather murmured. "I don't know why I bothered inviting you. I should have asked Durrell from the start."

The hair on the back of my neck stood up. What was all the fuss about Durrell? They hung out at one party. *One.* That didn't warrant replacing me.

"It's an emergency. I promise, I'll explain later," I mumbled. "Would you get me a playbill or something? Autographed would be awesome."

"Yeah. Okay. *If* I have time."

I swallowed hard. "See you on Monday?"

"Sure," Heather said. Then there was silence. She hung up.

"You didn't need to cancel your trip," Robbie said softly.

"Yeah. I did." Although Robbie was the last person I wanted to talk with, I needed to talk with someone. "Doesn't matter. She's freaking going to ask Durrell to go with her."

"Durrell? Like our teammate Durrell?"

"The one and only."

"Go with her where?" Robbie asked cautiously.

I hesitated. "We were going to see *Phantom* on Broadway."

Robbie wrinkled his nose. "What's he doing going to a pansy-ass musical?" He paused, then added, "Uh. No offense."

Offense taken.

"Uh, if it makes you feel better, he's probably only going so he can get some," Robbie said.

I stared at him. "How the hell would that make me feel better?"

"I don't know." Immediately after, Robbie added, "Maybe he likes her for real or something. That'd be better, right? I mean, it was his idea to go to hers to party. I could see him going out with her for a long time. He's seriously the type that would marry a high school girlfriend. I can picture it now—a glimpse into his life produced by TSN, him and Heather on a couch with three kids and a rescued Rottweiler saying that they fell for each other over a Broadway show."

I gritted my teeth. "Robbie? Do me a favor?"

"Yeah. Sure. Anything."

"Stop talking."

"But—"

"Just stop."

I turned my back to Robbie. I didn't want to think about Heather going on a date with Durrell when I was supposed to be going to that show. Durrell probably disliked musicals as much as I disliked him at that moment, though that dislike would fade. Durrell was too cool to stay angry at. He probably didn't even know I liked her. After all, I didn't exactly tell him when he asked. If I had, he probably wouldn't have bothered. He had integrity.

So why didn't I tell him, "Actually, I like her. A lot," when I had the chance?

I hugged my arms around my waist. I thought about Miss Maroney telling me to make my characters fall in love. For a moment, I pretended my arms were Heather. That we weren't best friends so we could get together.

Yeah, right.

10

Heather wasn't at her locker Monday morning. She didn't answer any of my texts either, not even the ones where I asked how the show was. I didn't like using my cell during school, even though most of the kids at Briar Rose did without consequence—I guess that's a perk of a private school geared for young professionals—but I peeked right after World Civilizations IV. Nothing.

I glanced toward Robbie's locker. He kept his head ducked, jerking out a textbook before heading to his next class. Beneath hooded lids, his eyes were flat and lifeless as buttons. He hadn't been himself—not that I was any expert on what that was anymore—since the knife incident. He wouldn't talk to me; and yet more than once, trapped so close in our room, I'd been startled out of daydreaming or some menial task, certain he'd been screaming at me.

Turning off my phone, I went to my next class.

Calculus was easy. I liked having foolproof formulas to work on. I was able to think about other things as I filled in the numbers and figured out the solution. I wanted to think about the dolphin people in my story, or maybe start a new one.

Instead, I thought about Robbie.

Identical twins were supposed to share so much, but we might as well have not been related. Sure, we came from the same split egg, but we were water and oil. We looked the same under a rolling boil, but we didn't mix.

If he were thinking about hurting himself, would I even know? A hundred times already I'd convinced myself he was fine, that if he wanted me to stick my nose in his business, he'd say something. I'd pretended everything was okay when Robbie laughed, ignoring how plastic his smiles could be.

"Is everything all right?"

My teacher, Mrs. Benedict, stopped by my desk. I looked around, unable to remember what I was just working on. It took staring at the pencil I gripped tightly to realize that I hadn't stopped after the nine assigned problems, but went through the next few pages of work as well.

"Yeah, sorry." I felt the sting of something acidic in my throat. "Um. Just . . . a lot on my mind."

"If you need a moment . . ." Her voice trailed off. Mrs. Benedict wasn't a kind woman by disposition. She was always fair to me and basically left me alone because I did what I was told and did well on exams, but she was never as warm as she was now. It was kind of pathetic that my teachers were more concerned about my well-being than my own parents.

"It's better that I keep busy, if that makes sense?"

She seemed to understand. At least her eyes seemed like they did. Mrs. Benedict patted me on the shoulder. "If you need anything . . ." Again, her voice trailed off.

I nodded, for a moment wishing she would hug me the way Mom wouldn't. I wondered how much attention I'd get if I broke down and confessed that something was seriously wrong with my brother. He kept saying I wasn't listening, but I was, I just didn't understand. Something happened at that practice, something more than losing a stupid drill.

I zoned through all my classes except for acting. Heather

wasn't there. Had she called in sick? Ms. Price approached me. "I hope I'll see you at the auditions this afternoon, Tristan."

My stomach dropped. The audition.

Of course, I'd been preparing something half-against my will, telling myself it was okay to practice because I didn't have to show up. Somehow, with *Phantom* and Robbie and everything else, I'd forgotten it was *this* Monday. Heather hadn't mentioned it at all—but there was no way she would miss it, right?

By lunch, I figured she had to be sick. Still, I sent her a text that said, *I think I'm really gonna do the audition today.* No response. Unusual.

I went into the cafeteria and saw the Gay-Bros eating their lunch. Craig caught my eye and waved before turning back to the others, clearly in the middle of a heated discussion, maybe another one about whether Hugh Jackman was secretly gay or not (spoiler alert: no one cares). I thought about sitting with the Gay-Bros, but some of those debates were draining and I didn't want anyone on the team to get the wrong idea. I'm pretty sure everyone knew I was straight, but locker room homophobia could make anyone's life miserable.

Finally, I sat down at the normal table—it was empty. No friends, no Heather, just me. It was . . . weird.

Halfway through lunch, I spotted her. She was sitting with some of the girls next to Durrell and some of the guys on the team. I dumped my tray without finishing my lunch, then walked to their table. "Hey," I greeted with a smile and wave. Immediately, Durrell put his arm around Heather's shoulder.

"Oh. Tristan. Hi." Heather smiled, but it seemed strangely icy.

"I didn't know you were in school today. You weren't at our table," I said, gesturing over my shoulder. "No one was."

"Oh . . . well, yeah. Just seemed kind of silly to not be

eating with Durrell since we're together, you know? I mean, that'd be weird," Heather said, words smooth as silk, like I should have known this would happen. My eyes honed in on Durrell's thumb as it rubbed her shoulder. "I mean, wouldn't you eat lunch with your girlfriend if you had one?"

Uh, ouch?

"Didn't save me a spot?" I tried to joke. "Not like I'm not on the team." She shifted in her seat, rubbed the back of her neck, twisted a curly lock of hair around her index and middle fingers.

"It's cramped," Durrell said abruptly, putting his backpack on an empty chair. I took a step backward. The hell was going on? Durrell was always the cool guy. And now, all of my teammates were giving me weird looks. I'd rather they treated me like I was still invisible.

Keisha interrupted, "We could pull up another chair if we all scoot in—"

Heather looked at Keisha, lips pursed together, eyes narrowing. A silent language between girls. Keisha withdrew and looked at her lap.

I cleared my throat. "Did I do something?"

No one answered. That usually meant yes.

My eyes moved two tables over. My brother turned his head and caught my eye. I saw his lips move, but couldn't read them. I looked away from him and at Heather. I tried to shrug it off. "It's uh . . . it's fine. Just was saying hi, you know? Let's uh . . . let's talk later."

"Yeah. Okay," she said hurriedly.

"I really want to—"

"I heard you the first time."

Double ouch. I gave a closed-mouthed smile before I made to leave.

"Wait," Keisha murmured, extending her hand toward me, but Heather slapped it down. I pretended I didn't notice as I left their table and returned to the empty one, just like how I pretended not to hear Keisha say, "It's not right, and you know it." Or Durrell say, "He's lucky he's on the team or I'd take care of it."

Maybe it was just one off-day, I tried to convince myself. Just one day of weirdness that I didn't understand. But even then I knew it wouldn't be the same.

11

My sheet music was getting wrinkled. I shifted my weight from foot to foot. Auditioning was probably a terrible idea. An insanely bad one. I'd talked myself in and out of going several times just standing in the hallway. If my parents found out, they'd kill me. If my teammates found out, which they would eventually, they'd rip on me like no one's business.

With a deep breath, I walked down the hallway toward the band room where the auditions would be held. I could at least stick my head in. Maybe decide then whether I'd have the balls to go through with it or not.

Halfway there, I saw my brother in the hallway with Raiden and two girls I didn't know. One was practically straddling Raiden's leg as they made out; the other was trying to press up against Robbie, who kept moving away and saying, "Knock it off." A chill rushed through my body. Something wasn't right. Robbie turned his head and our eyes met. His held the same fear he'd been drowning in last Saturday. My breath slowed.

My hands clenched around my sheet music. I dampened my lips. Robbie was *not* okay, but the audition was now. I'd made it this far, and it'd only be for a few minutes, not hours.

I could turn back. I knew I could. I could go home with Robbie and make sure he was fine.

But I stayed home with Robbie when I could have gone out with Heather. And now, things were messed up with me and her and the guys on the hockey team.

I studied my brother. He was with Raiden. He wouldn't do anything in front of Raiden. I was certain of that.

With a shaky breath, I continued to the band room. It'd only be a few hours. I could do the audition—in, out, fast—and be home just in case. For once, I had to do something that was just for me. He'd be fine. It'd be fine.

THE CLOSER it got to my call time, the more my stomach twisted. Pressure rose behind my sternum the way it always did before I threw up. I sipped a small bottle of coconut water. A lot of actors on Twitter swore by it, saying it helped lubricate their throats and produce crisper sounds. I hoped that was true. Not just because I wanted to sing better, but because it tasted rancid.

Behind the closed door, I heard Craig's muted voice singing "Color My World" from *Priscilla: Queen of the Desert*. After a roar of laughter, I wondered if he danced his way through the vocal. I wouldn't be surprised. Once he twerked on the Assistant Dean's car and didn't even get detention after setting off the alarm with his butt. He just couldn't keep from moving.

The door swung open. Craig sauntered out wearing the shortest shorts I'd ever seen and an open shirt. Both were a hideous shade of yellow.

"Holy . . . Tristan?" Craig asked, eyebrows raising. "You're not auditioning, are you?"

"Ms. Price talked me into it."

"Holy guacamole!" His face lit up as he pulled me in a hug. "So proud of you."

"Don't be proud yet. I could suck."

"Um, of course, I'm proud. Takes massive balls to audition."

"Tristan," Ms. Price called from the open door. "Ready to go?"

I extracted myself from Craig's grasp and walked into the room, sheet music bunched up in hand. Just inside the door, I felt a sharp pain around my neck. My body jerked involuntarily.

"You all right?" Ms. Price asked.

There was a throbbing in my ears and a weight on my chest. If this was stage fright, it fucking sucked. I forced a smile and approached the pianist to give her my sheet music. She quirked her brow, but said nothing.

Ms. Price sat on a folding chair. She adjusted a video camera on a tripod. The red recording light went on. "You want to say your name and who you're auditioning for before you start?"

"I didn't realize this was going to be recorded."

"Is that a problem?"

"I . . . no." I gazed into the eye of the camera. "I'm, uh, I'm Tristan Betterby and I'll be singing 'Pity the Child' from *Chess.*"

Ms. Price quirked her brow. "You do know *The Drowsy Chaperone's* a comedy, right?"

My face darkened, fingers curling against my palm. Talk about a stupid choice of song. After all, Craig did something campy and fun. Probably everyone was doing something campy and fun. It was just that "Pity the Child" meant something to me. The first time I watched the 2008 live recording, I became speechless when Adam Pascal sang. The kind of raw talent that earned him the lead in *Rent* even though he had no formal training. I thought maybe it'd be a good luck charm.

"I've never auditioned before," I mumbled.

"Don't worry about it. I don't want you to get nervous," Ms. Price said.

Little late for that.

When I heard the piano, I had to take a moment's pause. My voice started low, maybe a touch shaky. The red glare of the camera pierced my eyes, expanding until I couldn't see anything else. I was deaf to my words, hearing only a loud, static hum. A sudden bitterness burst forth with each unheard accusation. Once I hit the final "Who?" the static cleared. My own voice, crystal clear, pitch perfect, rang out as I hung desperately onto the last note.

The pianist stared at me, as did Ms. Price.

"Holy shit," Ms. Price said. "You did half of that *acapella*."

What?

My cheeks were wet. I turned my head and used my sleeve to wipe away tears I hadn't realized were there. Had the pianist stopped? Had I gone past my twenty measures and continued, lost in the moment?

I swallowed hard, unable to remember a single thing about my song. How it sounded, if I had conviction. Anything except that last note. "Was it . . . was it okay?"

"Not only did you sing it *acapella*, but you held the end note for twenty-three beats," Ms. Price said. *"Twenty-three beats.* You seriously haven't studied with anyone before? *Anyone?"*

"Just, uh . . . just what I told you. With Heather."

"It's like you're Adam Pascal the second." And, for a moment, I felt the same sort of swelling pride and incoherence Robbie did whenever he was referred to Wayne Gretzky. Ms. Price folded her arms and continued, "You know, when Adam Pascal started, he got a lot of criticism for his notes. His voice was weak except for the gravel. But that's something he worked on. That's something *you* can work on." She took a breath, head cocked to the side as if she was debating. "I want to make a few phone calls. See if I can get you some additional training."

"I uh . . . my parents are making me do hockey."

"You don't do hockey year round, do you?"

I looked at the card and swallowed. "How much is it going to cost me?"

Ms. Price almost laughed. "Oh. Oh, no, Tristan. This would be *pro bono*. Just like dance lessons at my studio."

I spluttered a bit. "My parents are kinda crazy and not supportive of this stuff, but I want to take you up on that. I mean, if you're serious. Just . . . might have to wait until the semester's over. Is that too late?"

"I'm pretty sure I've got a few friends who would wait for the chance to train a voice like yours. And I'd love to get you in my studio dancing with Craig."

"You teach Craig outside of school?"

"Who do you think got him enrolled here?" Ms. Price then asked, "I don't mean to embarrass you, but are you wearing a belt?"

I shook my head and glanced to my jeans. "No, I didn't wear—"

"I mean a dance belt. Not a belt-belt."

"What's a dance belt?"

"If I didn't know you hadn't had any formal training before, now I would." Ms. Price scribbled down a list and handed it to me. "Before you work with me, make sure you get the following." I looked over it: three dance belts, two jazz pants, five white T-shirt, two black shorts.

I shook my head. "I can't believe you're offering to help me for free. This is just . . ." I couldn't help it. I pressed my hand to my face as I tried not to cry. It was happening so fast. It was overwhelming.

Arms wrapped around me. Ms. Price squeezed me close, giving me the contact I craved. "You might have had a late start, but it's not too late. Don't waste this chance."

"I won't. I swear, I won't."

"Then we're even."

IN THE lobby, everyone started cheering, led by Craig, now dressed in outdoor winter clothes. "Holy CRAP. Tristan, that was amazeballs."

"You heard me?"

"Everyone did."

I looked around the hall. I recognized almost everyone from theatre, but I didn't see Heather. "I chose the wrong song."

"She had you stay in for *fifteen minutes.* You booked a lead."

"No way," I said, shaking my head. "She was being nice."

"People don't do nice in theatre," Craig said with a little grin, looping his arm around my back after I put on my coat. "Seriously, that was awesome."

Awesome—a word associated with Robbie.

Awesome—a word never associated with me. At least not until now.

Awesome—my new favorite word in the dictionary.

Awesome—me.

12

When I got home and walked through the front door, the air was thick. Hard to breathe, like walking past a smoker. The *thud-thud* of my heartbeat pounded in my ears. I moved toward the stairs and glanced at the living room. Mom and Dad were sitting in their chairs. Mom had a box of tissues on her lap and a plastic grocery bag filled with used ones to her side. Robbie sat on the couch across from them, hugging his knees to his chest, hiding his face.

"Tristan," Dad said, his voice a low growl, "come in here."

I stopped just outside the room, not setting foot on the living room's cream carpet. When Robbie and I were kids we used to play "the floor is lava." Did we get along then? We must have, but I couldn't remember.

Mom asked, "Where were you?"

I shifted, waiting to see whether Mom wanted an answer or not, before saying, "Study group."

"Bullshit." Dad's voice always scared me when it dropped to this register. Sometimes it was followed by the fists Robbie inherited. "Where were you?"

I looked at the floor and inhaled slowly. As quietly as I could, I said, "At an audition."

"What'd you say?"

I barely raised my voice. "I was at an audition, for a musical."

Mom burst to her feet. Her face was dark red. "You did *what?*" I took a step back. I'd expected a big reaction from Dad; Mom barely looked up from her mobile. Dad was the one who yelled at us, but that yelling was always related to hockey. Even he seemed taken aback by Mom's outburst.

"I'm sorry," I spluttered. "The show starts when the season's over. I thought—"

"You thought what, Tristan?" Mom took a step toward me. Her mascara was wet around her eyes, making them darker. "You said acting was an easy elective."

"It is. I just—"

"You're just like him," Mom murmured. I shrank back. Who was *him?* Uncle Anthony? But she broke from that reverie with a sneer. "What's next? You're going to tell us you're a homo?"

My twin's head snapped up. He stared at me wide-eyed.

"No!" I said, shaking my head. "No, Mom, I—"

"Is that it? Is that why you went over to Heather's so often? Why you don't have a girlfriend?"

"No!"

Mom advanced toward me until I was pressed against the wall with nowhere to turn. "What's next? You want to be some sort of woman? You want to be Caitlyn Jenner?"

"That's enough," Dad said, rising to his feet.

Dad and Mom stared at each other before Mom sat down, folding her arms across her chest. Dad looked down at me. "So, you decided to audition for a play instead of come home with your brother?"

"Yes, sir," I whispered. I didn't dare correct him with "musical."

"You were supposed to watch Robbie."

"I thought that was just overnight . . ."

Robbie's shoulders started to shake. Before the knife incident, the last time I saw Robbie cry was when we were nine and our dog was hit by a car. Robbie cried for days then, and wouldn't even consider getting another pet even though I wanted one. Now he was on the verge of a breakdown for the second time in a week.

Dad's enormous fist snaked around my bicep. It hurt. He hauled me up the stairs. Immediately, Robbie was on his feet, chasing after us.

"Dad, don't!"

The hair on the back of my neck stood up. Robbie was never the type to beg.

"It's not Tristan's fault! Me being a screw up has *nothing* to do with him!"

But Dad didn't slow, dragging me behind him toward my room. I wondered if he was going to beat me, how he used to when he still thought I could be good and just wasn't trying hard enough. The day he stopped doing that, I was almost disappointed. It meant he gave up on me.

Dad yanked me into my room. In the center of the floor was the ceiling fan, broken and bent, with bits of crumbled ceiling around it. I looked up to the hole and electrical wiring. "What happened?"

"Your brother tried to hang himself."

The air to my windpipe cut off like Dad's words had turned a tap. The room seemed engulfed in a silent explosion, something so big I became deaf. My throat burned.

An image came to my mind. Robbie on the top bunk with sheets around his neck, trembling before shoving himself off.

I felt the cracking and collision as he hit the ground, the fan landing on top of him.

I doubled over, put a hand over my mouth. Dad was screaming at me, but I still felt deaf to everything except, "Your brother tried to hang himself."

I didn't even realize I was dragged back down the stairs and into the living room until Dad pushed me on the couch. My head hit the back. I trembled, pressing myself into the cushions. This couldn't have been real. I just went out for an audition. I was only gone for a couple of hours. Maybe three, tops. Probably two.

This was preventable.

This was my fault.

Robbie stood by the couch, disheveled, body swallowed by his large, black hoodie. He held his forearm over his eyes to hide his tears. *Hockey players don't cry.* Dad had drilled that into our heads since we were four. Robbie tried to sniff back his snot, then rubbed the back of his hoodie sleeve over his red nose to wipe it away.

"It's not Tristan's fault." I wanted him to be quiet. Defending me made me feel even worse. "I messed up. I screwed up."

"Robbie, just shut up," Dad snarled, though it wasn't the sort of yell that came with anger. It was the kind that was born from terror. Dad was afraid. Afraid of what Robbie might do, what he could have done.

Dad turned his fury on me. "You can say goodbye to hanging out with your friends for a while."

"And you're not doing musicals under this roof," Mom added.

My twin tried again. "Mom, Dad, don't—"

"Shut up, Robbie. Just . . . shut up." Dad suddenly choked. I'd never seen him so close to tears. Robbie was their child, their special child. Their favorite son. Were they like this when Robbie came out breach at birth? Or was it only after they realized just how promising Robbie's future was? Every little change was monumental in their eyes, from his bleached hair to his fake lip piercing, which Grandpa had said looked like a fish caught on some jerkbait. "That's the point," Robbie had told him.

Dad exhaled. He glanced at Mom, who glared daggers at me. "While your mother and I take care of the mess, you're to clean the rest of the house downstairs, Tristan. Understood?"

"Yes, sir."

Mom picked up the tissue box and carried it with her. She left the grocery bag with used tissues behind. The sound of their upstairs door closing didn't mute anything as they began to scream.

"It's not like Tristan's going to end up like Anthony," my dad yelled.

"Yes, he will!"

"Even if he was, it wouldn't matter! As long as it's not Robbie."

"Oh, so just because Tristan won't be drafted it doesn't matter? You're a real bastard."

"Go to hell!"

I stood next to my twin in silence. A tear rolled down my cheek before I could wipe it away. Robbie looked at the ceiling, narrowed his eyes, and stuck his middle finger up.

I trudged to the kitchen where our supply closet was. Robbie's footsteps tapped behind me. "You want to help or are you going to call me queer, too?" I mumbled, unsure how

I could apologize to Robbie for my negligence. It felt like I was only now regaining my hearing after the explosion and looking at the bloody carnage around me.

Robbie reached around me from behind with a sudden, tight hold. At first, I jerked, hands gripping onto his wrists. He was going to strangle me. Choke me until I passed out.

But Robbie's hands didn't move near my neck. They hugged my stomach. He rested his head on the back of my shoulders. My shirt became wet. He started to shake, hard.

"Robbie?" I whispered, afraid to move.

"I'm so . . . so sorry, Tristan," Robbie murmured. "That's so shitty of them."

"Doesn't matter."

"It *does* matter," he insisted. He stalled and squeezed tighter. "If you're gay—"

"I'm not," I said as I pulled from his grasp and faced him. "I just like musicals. That doesn't mean I'm gay."

"You're sure?"

"You really think there aren't hetero men who like musicals?"

"No, I just—" Robbie bit his lip. Frustrated with words he couldn't formulate, he grabbed the mop and bucket. At a time like this, that telekinetic stuff so many identical twins talk about would be helpful.

We cleaned in silence for several minutes. Finally, I asked, "Why'd you do it?"

Robbie kept his eyes low. "Sometimes you get an idea in your head and you don't think about consequences." He pulled the neck of his hoodie down enough for me to see the bruising and raw skin around his neck. I finally processed the cuts on his face and purple swelling around his eyes, probably from where the fan came crashing down.

"Dad hasn't decided what my excuse to Coach is this time. Probably something heroic, like me falling down while shoving a little kid out of the way of a moving car."

Robbie looked like he was waiting for me to say something, but I kept my mouth shut. Nothing I could say would be worthwhile. Nothing would take back the horrible mistake I had made.

As we cleaned, we listened to the sounds of our parents rearranging furniture. I wondered what the room would look like, what we were doomed for next. Would everything look the same as it was? The only thing I was sure about was that this time I'd take it with my head down.

13

My room was sealed. Literally. Boarded up with long nails like it was a condemned building. It didn't seem real.

In Robbie's room, our mattresses now lay side-by-side, taking up almost the entire room. We didn't even get box springs. Our table was still there, only about a foot away from the mattresses. Even squeezing between the table and a computer chair would be hard. On the desk, the scissors were gone. So were the stapler and paper cutter. In the closet, the clothing bar was missing as well as the door. Our nice suits lay flat on the floor wrapped in plastic. The room was stuffy and suffocating. Even though it was freezing, I opened the window the whole way.

Cold air flooded the room, making it less claustrophobic. Shivering, I leaned out and inhaled. The chill air cleared my nostrils and my mind. Robbie stepped up next to me. He fidgeted with the drawstrings on the neck of his hoodie. "I keep making things worse."

"Don't."

"No, really. This was on me."

"No. It wasn't. If I hadn't auditioned—"

"You really think you could have stopped me?"

I pulled my head back in the room. "You don't?"

Robbie didn't answer.

I crossed the room to our table and tugged at my desk chair. It caught on the mattress. The front of the table pressed against my stomach as I squeezed in, but I didn't budge. I needed to listen to music and write.

I turned on Spotify but couldn't find any music to help me relax. Instead, I put on *Billy Elliot* and listened to "Angry Dance" on loop at least ten times, then put on *Heathers,* mouthing along to "Life Boat." Other people's hopelessness made me feel a little less alone, I guess.

Even with an open Word document, my creativity was as dry as the last Florida Panthers' goal drought. Working on my dolphin story would be impossible.

I took out one of my textbooks but didn't read a single word. My mind kept drifting to Robbie, only hours ago, trying to hang himself in my room while I auditioned. I touched my throat. Hadn't I felt a raw pain right before I sang? Wasn't there a nagging feeling that something was wrong—really wrong—that I ignored? A warning.

Robbie sat next to me, with his headphones on, in some sort of chat room. I didn't even know there were chat rooms anymore—I thought those pretty much died when people switched to cable modems.

After a few minutes, Robbie got up and mostly shut the window, leaving just a small crack for ventilation. I glanced over at his screen, but it was minimized.

That night I couldn't sleep. I stared at Robbie's blanket-covered feet; he slept in the opposite direction from me. I thought about us in the womb, how Robbie was born breach, the opposite of me. Now was no different in this confined space.

Robbie rolled on his mattress. "Hey, Tristan? You awake?"

"Yeah."

"I can't sleep."

"Same."

My brother sat upright, his body a silhouette. "Can I tell you something?"

"Uh. Okay?" I propped myself up on my elbows.

"Things might be a little messed up soon. Just so you have a heads-up."

"What do you mean?"

Robbie hesitated. In the darkness of the room, I couldn't make out his expression. Was he upset? Lonely? Scared?

"I think I really screwed up."

"Screwed up what?"

Robbie's tone changed. "Coach said the director of scouting from St. Louis was talking to him for about an hour about me."

"Holy shit. The Blues are interested in you?"

"Maybe. Seems like more western conference teams are kicking tires right now. Coach said Colorado, Calgary, and Vancouver are supposed to watch the next one. Possibly a bunch of others. They could be looking at Beau, Durrell, or Raiden, though."

"You know they're looking at you."

". . . yeah. I know." Robbie reached under his pillow for a slip of paper. "This morning, Dad gave me this."

I picked up the sheet and reached for my iPhone. Using it as a light, I read the sheet of paper:

CALLED—POSSIBLE DRAFT COMBINE INTERVIEWS?

1. *Calgary Flames—10 calls*
2. *Anaheim Ducks—7 calls*
3. *Vancouver Canucks—5 calls*
4. *Arizona Coyotes—5 calls*
5. *Colorado Avalanches—3 calls*
6. *Minnesota Wild—2 calls*

7. *Washington Capitals—2 calls*

8. *Winnipeg Jets—1 call*

9. *Los Angeles Kings—1 call*

10. *Chicago Blackhawks—1 call*

11. *Detroit Redwings—1 call*

12. *Florida Panthers—1 call*

13. *New Jersey Devils—1 call (returned)*

I looked up at Robbie as I turned off the cellphone light. "This is legit?"

"I don't think Dad would lie about it to inflate my ego."

"Oh my God." I couldn't help it. A huge smile spread across my face. "Robbie, this is seriously incredible. I mean, holy crap. That many teams *already?*"

"Dad said it's not enough," Robbie mumbled.

I stared at him. "Robbie, *thirteen teams* have called about you. *Thirteen* out of *thirty.* I mean, you can't even schedule interviews until two weeks before combine. That number should go up. And even if it didn't, that's incredible. Look how many times Calgary called about you!"

"Yeah, but Dad keeps reminding me that the Devils only called once."

"Yeah, but they called."

"Because Dad called them first," Robbie mumbled.

"You think Dad would be upset if you got drafted by a different team?"

Robbie thought about it for a few moments. "No," he said. "I just need to hold it together long enough to make sure I get drafted."

"Why are you even worried?"

"I told you, I think I really screwed up." Robbie's voice dropped, "You know, the guys could beat the crap out of me.

Wouldn't matter if I wear an A on my jersey. If they found out, it'd be the end. Just one less person to compete with for a scout's attention."

I sat upright, pressing my hands on the mattress. "Why would the guys try to beat you up just because a scout's looking at you?"

"They don't know, Tristan."

"Don't know what?"

"Forget it." Robbie pulled the sheet of paper from me and shoved it under his pillow. He abruptly rolled on his mattress so his back faced me. I frowned.

"Robbie? What don't they know?"

"Nothing," he mumbled. I stayed still, not sure whether I should try to say something else or remain quiet.

When the sound of Robbie's breathing pattern change, I got up and squeezed into the space between my chair and table. My mind wouldn't slow. Robbie should have been in therapy. My parents didn't even take him to the ER this time just in case that'd get on his record. Like his mental health would lower his draft value.

I pulled up my story of the dolphin people, particularly focusing on the kids who were in the hut by themselves, biting my lower lip the way Robbie always did as I resumed typing.

There was something strange happening on the island. You could feel it in the air. It became harder to breathe. Each inhale was a labored huff-huff. Clouds rolled in, thick and low to the ground. Sluggish. The huts were shrinking, but the dolphin people remained the same size. Their homes constricted around their long bodies. Soon, their heads and feet were sticking out of the hut until they were stuck.

From the center of the island, black beasts emerged from beneath the sand like crabs. They dripped black blood from their teeth. It's suppertime, they said, then began to whack off the dolphin people's heads with a machete, like a butcher. Mercilessly, they killed all of the dolphin people and kids, except two. Brothers. They had grown too large, or the hut shrank too small around them. The black beasts put collars on their slick necks with metal chains tied to a stake in the ground.

A whimpering sound drew my attention. I saved the story, then went back to my mattress. Robbie was crying in his sleep. I wasn't sure whether I should wake him up or let him sleep through it.

Carefully, I rested my hand on his side. He jerked once, and I withdrew. His body stilled.

I pulled my blankets up and turned on my side, my back toward Robbie. A draft crept along the floor from the open crack in the window. I curled my body into itself as I thought about my brother, not surprised when the next morning we woke to a sheet of white on the ground. Snow.

14

Despite Robbie's bitching, I talked him into going to school half an hour early so I could wait outside Heather's locker. The second she made eye contact with me, she half-looked like she wanted to walk the other way but thought better of it.

"What do you want?" Heather asked.

"We need to talk."

"I don't have time."

"He tried it again," I said urgently.

"Who tried what again?"

I gazed at Heather. "You know."

"No. I don't."

"Robbie," I said.

She took a few moments, then groaned. "You're joking."

"Why would I joke about that?"

"Why didn't you text me?"

"Because I *can't*." I rubbed the back of my neck. "You know when I had to cancel on seeing *Phantom* with you? I think I stopped him in time. He went like all crazy with a kitchen knife."

"Why didn't you tell me?"

"Because you've been avoiding me."

"I haven't—"

"Yes. You have. Lunch—"

"I want to sit with my boyfriend. Is that a crime?"

"You wouldn't even pull up a chair for me!" I closed my eyes. "I hate this. We're supposed to be best friends, not like . . . this."

"We wouldn't be like this if you'd actually talk to me."

"I'm telling you everything I can."

"Not everything." Heather opened her locker and rummaged through it. Her lips pursed. "You didn't even tell me you were auditioning. A text message the day of? Seriously?"

I paused. "Is that what this is about? I didn't think I needed to ask your permission."

"You don't think I'd support you going for an ensemble role?"

"I was nervous, okay?" I laughed uncomfortably. "My audition was so bad at the beginning. I picked the wrong song. Wrong genre, everything. She let me sing that, but had me stay in for fifteen minutes."

Heather's lips twisted a bit. "You stayed for fifteen minutes at your audition?"

"Yeah. I think it was pity."

Heather seemed to weigh a few ideas in her head. Then she flashed a warmer smile. "You know, you're right. We really should fix this awkwardness between us. I'm willing to give you another chance to make it right."

I braved a smile and nodded. "That . . . uh. That sounds good." Although I wasn't entirely convinced that I was the one who needed to make things right.

"We'll be a dynamite duo in acting again."

"That sounds amazing." My face lit up. "Really, whatever you want. Duets, dialogues, you name it."

Heather's smile broadened. It drew me in, the way it always did. I leaned down to hug her. She hugged back with one arm, a little stiffly, then pulled away. "I gotta go."

"Yeah, sure, no problem."

I watched her hurry down the hall to Durrell. I smiled and waved; Durrell nodded his head. When Heather hugged him, she stood on her toes and whispered something in his ear. Durrell's expression changed. Sort of like his eyes were narrowing at me.

I headed in the direction of World Civilizations IV, but slowed by the theatre. Keisha stood outside the door, staring at a piece of paper. "Hey," I greeted.

Keisha whirled on me, wiping her eyes. My smile disappeared. "What's wrong?"

"Nothing," she said with a forced laugh. "Just, uh, just saw the cast list. But forget that. I didn't even get to say congratulations yet. Craig said you were auditioning for ensemble, so talk about a promotion."

"What are you talking about?"

Keisha stepped aside and pointed to the list.

MAN IN CHAIR—JEFF CARSON
THE CHAPERON—ELISA O'NEILL
JANET—HEATHER STONE
ROBERT—TRISTAN BETTERBY

The rest of the cast list blurred as I took a step back.

"Congratulations," Keisha reiterated, smile warm and broad and encouraging.

"I—how?" I asked, a little stunned.

"You're good," Keisha said.

"I don't even tap—"

"Yeah, but you play hockey. I mean, how incredible will it be to have a Robert who actually skates?"

"You think that's why I got the part?"

"I think you got the part because you're really good," Keisha said.

I looked down the list again, noticed how Craig booked Aldolpho—a nearly perfect cast with Aldolpho's flamboyant characterization—then lower.

"I don't see your name," I said.

"Ensemble," Keisha said softly. "Anyone not on this gets to be in the ensemble."

"Oh." Suddenly, getting cast as Robert was a bit less exciting, especially as Keisha tried to hide her disappointment and the lingering hint of tears.

"I just—" Keisha laughed uncomfortably. "It's stupid, but I really wanted to be Janet."

"Janet?" That was a surprise. "I didn't think she was your type of character at all."

"Clearly she's not since I wasn't cast as her."

"I didn't mean that—"

"I didn't mean it like that either, I swear," Keisha said quickly. "Just . . . sometimes I wonder." She looked at me. "You'd tell it to me straight if I asked you something, right?"

"If I can, I mean."

"It's just because of talent, right?" Her face was strained. "I mean, you don't think that I didn't get Janet because I'm black, right?"

I shook my head. "No. Ms. Price is cool. I don't think . . . I *really* don't think she'd turn you down because of that."

"So, I wasn't good enough."

"I didn't mean—"

"I know. Heather was better. She got cast as Janet. I made ensemble. It doesn't mean my career's over."

"For what it's worth, I think you're a hell of a singer."

Keisha gave me a closed-lipped smile. "Heather's lucky to have you as her leading man."

She turned from me, hustling down the hallway. I was taken aback. What was that about? I looked at the board and frowned. Was me liking Heather really that obvious? And why would Keisha care? Keisha couldn't like me. We barely knew each other.

Still, as I left for my first class, my chest ached a bit. Something was wrong about all of this. More wrong since I didn't know what exactly was so wrong, or why it felt so wrong, and that wrongness bothered me throughout my classes, through acting, through lunch, through the end of the day, and through hockey practice. That sort of wrongness that didn't quite fade.

15

Robbie and I headed to Heather's house as soon as we got off the team bus after a great away-win. Robbie absolutely slaughtered the Bricktown Bulldogs, getting a hat trick in the first period—but, alas, no hats on the ice, with the whole away high school hockey thing—then a fourth goal in the third period. I actually got an assist on his second goal, too. For once, I kind of felt bad that we weren't going to be able to hang out with the guys, especially since Robbie looked so happy.

Durrell drove Heather in his car while I followed in mine with Robbie, taking the roads slowly. The snow had melted quickly, too quickly, and the rapid change in temperature made the streets extra slippery. We crossed the soggy lawn to where Heather and Durrell stood on the porch by the front door. "You know why the rest of the guys didn't come?" Robbie asked. "A bunch of them were free. And I mean, I'm sure they would have paid for beer and pizza."

"They weren't invited, and I didn't feel like beer and pizza," Heather said as she led us into the kitchen, pulling out bags of Doritos and cans of Pepsi. "Private party."

From behind me, I thought I heard Robbie. *Memo to self: never hang with Tristan's lame ass friends. At least not without Raiden.*

"What about my friends?" I asked him, a little defensively.

Robbie quirked his brow. "I didn't say anything."

"You just said—" I cut myself off. Heather and Durrell looked just as confused as Robbie. I must have imagined it.

After stocking up on Pepsi and Doritos, we tromped up the steps to Heather's guest room with the two double beds. I hopped on one and looked at Heather. She sat on the other with Durrell. Robbie stared at the bed I was sitting on, swallowed, and sat on the floor, putting as much distance between the bed and himself.

"Figure we could all watch a movie," Heather said as she flipped through Netflix with her remote. She lingered over *Mean Girls* for a few seconds, then clicked through the dramas until she landed on *The Virgin Suicides.*

My chest tightened. My mind went to Robbie holding his hands over his mouth, foamy vomit spilling between his fingers. Then a grainy, flickering vision of him falling with a broken ceiling fan crashing down, like it was a film reel.

I asked, "Is there anything else we can put on? Something that's not a million years old and morbid?"

"I've been dying to watch it again. It's such a great movie," she said. I glanced at Durrell. I couldn't remind Heather about Robbie's suicide attempts, not with him there, not when she wasn't supposed to know.

We locked eyes. My stomach sank. This was a test, something to see if I could make it up to her. So I said nothing.

The movie started. My attention moved to Robbie, who gripped his Pepsi tightly. After the first daughter committed suicide by jumping out of a window onto a spiked fence, his hand began to shake. My heart rate sped up.

"We could change movies. This one's kind of dragging," I said, trying to meet Heather's eye.

"It gets so good, though," Heather answered, not budging.

When the movie got to the part where the girls picked out

fabric to make their prom dresses, Heather said, "You know, the man who lived here before us committed suicide."

"Seriously?" Durrell asked, bewildered, maybe a little freaked out. I was caught off-guard too. Heather never mentioned this to me before. Not once.

"She's joking," I said, sitting up a bit straighter. I don't know why she was being this insensitive. Did Durrell's presence make her stupid?

"It's true," she insisted. "It's why we got the house so cheap. Hanged himself right here." Heather climbed on the twin beds, reached her hand to the ceiling, and touched the paint. Stroked it gently, like with a doting pet. She came back down and snuggled up to Durrell.

I turned away from her, then froze. Robbie was staring at the ceiling. Immediately, I moved from the bed to sit on the floor next to my brother. For a moment, I thought about touching his shoulder or patting his back, but I didn't. He'd take it the wrong way. Like I was patronizing him in one of those Public Service Announcements.

"You okay?" I whispered. Robbie's head snapped down. His pupils were dilated and hazy. "We can turn it off if you want. Put on something else."

He blinked, then smiled and shook his head. "No, it's cool. I want to know what happens."

"You sure? I'm not really enjoying it."

"I told you, I want to see what happens."

I looked back at Heather and Durrell, ready to insist we put on another movie, but stiffened. They were making out like we weren't even there, Heather straddling his lap as Durrell gripped her hips.

I grabbed the remote and hit stop. "If there's no objection, I'm putting on something else."

Heather and Durrell said nothing; they were still making out. Her shirt was snaking up in the back. I could see the red band of her bra.

"Do you guys want to order a pizza or anything? Chinese?" I asked, raising my voice. Heather opened her eye, glanced at me, then closed them to keep making out with Durrell. My chest felt like an anchor pulling my shoulders down.

It sucked being a third wheel, even though Robbie was there as well. Guess we were both just spare tires. Training wheels.

I nudged Robbie with my elbow and gestured with my head to the door. He looked at me. *You sure?*

Positive, I answered.

Quietly, we got up and walked out of the house. We crossed the lawn, our Converse sneakers getting soggy with each step. The temperature was dropping. It'd freeze overnight.

Robbie shoved his hands deep in the pockets of his hoodie after he got in the car. "I know she's your friend and all, but what a bitch. The making out in front of you and stuff," Robbie said. "I mean, even if she didn't know you had a complete boner for her, talk about needing to get a room. And what the hell's up with Durrell? Usually he's not such a douche canoe."

"I don't want to talk about this."

"But—"

"I said, I don't want to talk about it!" I snapped as I pulled onto the road. "None of this would have happened if you weren't a dick and didn't try to kill yourself."

I regretted the words the moment they came out. My resentment was a time bomb, years of holding back the words I wished to yell at Robbie. Words I never said out of the fear of him kicking the crap out of me. "I mean, why would you even want to kill yourself? You have *everything!*"

"Because I panicked and couldn't stop, okay!"

I hit the brakes so hard we jerked forward against our seat belts. I hadn't expected him to answer me, and certainly hadn't expected him to say something like that. The hell did Robbie mean? Robbie was fearless.

"Pull over," Robbie said. I hesitated. "Seriously. Pull over."

I moved the car to the side of the road and parked. Robbie got out and I followed him. He walked quickly, hands shoved deep in his hoodie's pockets. I followed him down a smooth path to the town park. We climbed up the steps to the gazebo. Robbie sat down. Hesitantly, I sat next to him. My twin rubbed his knees. "I hate being an outsider. It stresses me out. You're lucky with your theatre friends. You're all close and everything, you know?"

I didn't understand what he meant. "You have way more friends than me."

Robbie snorted. "Everyone's 'friends' when they're on a team together. It's like the army. You can't hate your squad because they're the ones saving your ass. But there's only so much space. Only so many jobs. You've got friends outside of hockey. I don't. You're lucky."

I rubbed the back of my neck. "I didn't realize you felt that alienated." He looked at me, almost hopefully. Like he was beckoning me to go on. "You seem happy enough." Although right after I said it, Robbie didn't seem happy. In fact, he hadn't seemed happy for a long time. I couldn't remember the last time he laughed. Truly laughed, not the fake laughs he forced out, part of the Robbie Betterby Hockey Star routine.

"If I wasn't expected to draft high, it'd be different." Robbie looked at his feet. "I have to keep a low profile."

Low profile?

I waited for my brother to elaborate, but he didn't. I shook my head. "I don't understand."

Robbie folded his arms across his chest and tilted his head back. "No one wants to hang around depressed people and get sucked into their mess. People who say they do lie, or they've got something seriously wrong in their brain. I mean, seriously, why would you go out of your way to hang out with someone who was completely miserable *all the time*? There's, like, obligation to watch out for your teammates and shit. If the guys got worried and started asking questions, I don't think I could lie. Just easier to keep it to myself, you know?"

What lie? What stuff?

Figuring out Robbie was nothing I ever attempted to do in the past. Before, he was just a hockey player. A damned good one who reeked confidence. Now, he was struggling to speak.

Thick clouds covered the stars and moon. The air was thick and heavy. It'd rain later. Almost inaudibly, Robbie said, "You have no clue how much I hate myself."

His words cut into me like the blade of a silent samurai. I felt the threatening prickle of unexpected tears in my eyes.

"Why?" I wanted to know. No, *needed* to know. How could someone who had our parents' undivided attention, the hockey team's most promising prospect, hate himself enough to want to die?

Robbie bit his lower lip, hung onto the fake piercing, like it'd make talking easier. Just like he was a fish caught on some jerkbait. I wanted to reel him in, but he kept fighting the line.

I asked again, "Why'd you try to kill yourself?"

Robbie took a long time to answer. "I don't know." Then, in a whirlwind, he said, "It was stupid. People do stupid shit when they're depressed. Even Raiden."

Raiden?

"Is that what's getting you?" I asked. "Are you worried that he's not going to get drafted or something? Or that he'd go to a division rival?"

"You really have no clue, do you?"

I would if you told me anything, I barely refrained from saying.

Robbie got to his feet. "Come on, let's go home. I've got something for you, anyway."

"What? Like a present?"

"Sort of. More like an 'I'm sorry for ruining your Broadway trip and accidentally getting Heather and Durrell together.'" He rubbed the back of his neck. "I found a torrent of some twenty-fifth anniversary of *The Phantom of the Opera* or some shit. Figured if you weren't there, you could at least see it."

He took off before I could confirm what I heard, or thank him. I hustled to catch up. Despite the threat of rain that would turn the snow to slush, the night felt almost refreshing. I never had a serious talk with my twin before. The closest we came was a year or two ago at dinner when he started talking about Tori Amos and Fiona Apple and how sad it was that so many recorded female vocalists were rape victims, since people capitalized off of women's trauma and misery. "Men are pigs," he had said, disgusted. "If I ever end up like that, just kill me." I'd asked him to pass the salt.

Now, we walked with our strides in almost perfect alignment. It was strange to remotely empathize with him, but I wasn't dumb enough to think one serious talk after eighteen years of not speaking would make us similar. We weren't. But maybe it'd teach us how to communicate. Maybe we'd understand each other the way twins were supposed to.

16

At Monday's practice, Durrell avoided me in the locker room. I hadn't seen him since he and Heather thought dry humping in front of us was an awesome idea. Anytime I tried to walk near him, he'd move across the room, picking up a piece of equipment, or going into the bathroom, or rushing out on the ice to work on a strained muscle. Maybe he was just embarrassed at getting carried away. I guess I could see that.

When I stepped on the ice, some of the guys gave me strange looks and a wide berth. When I shot a stray puck at the net as we loosened up, there was whispering behind me.

"Hey, Tristan. Wait up!" Smitty called as he skated up to me. He put his glove over his nose and mouth. "Oh my God. Your breath stinks."

"Ha, ha," I said dryly. "Like you didn't rip that from a Youtube video."

"I'm serious, though. Your breath smells like dick."

Smitty was across the ice before I even had a chance to respond.

We dropped to the ice with our legs spread, knees bent so our calves and feet stuck out in a W. I leaned forward to heighten the intensity of the abductor stretch, allowing gravity to split my legs further.

"You look like you're just waiting for someone to pound your ass," Durrell commented from behind me.

I turned to face him. "We're all stretching the same."

"None of us look like we're asking for it."

Some of the guys laughed. My cheeks flushed with anger. "Why are you staring at my ass anyway?" I snapped.

"It's in the way."

My brother skated next to me and dropped to one knee, stretching out his quads with a groan. "Oh. My. God. I seriously must have done something when I was sleeping. I'm sore as hell. What about you?"

I glanced at my brother. Beneath his breath, he said, "Ignore them."

Coach Benoit set up a course with traffic cones and various obstacles. He scribbled the exercise on a white board. We were to weave through, circle, change directions. A ladder was set on its side for us to work the puck through its grates. Robbie volunteered to go first.

Once Coach blew his whistle, it was like magic. Robbie was so light on his feet, it looked like he was tap dancing. He skated across the ice with ease, leaning into the turns and stick handling like he could have kept his eyes closed.

By the time Robbie finished, everyone was tapping their stick against the ice and hollering.

"Who's next?"

"Tristan wants to go," Durrell said suddenly.

I tensed up and shook my head. "It's okay. I'll wait."

"No, really. He's being shy," Smitty agreed. "Let him go."

"Butter, get up there," Coach Benoit said.

I hated doing any exercise after Robbie. It made me look even worse than I was. I took my spot and waited for the whistle. I skated quickly toward the first cone, taking the turn a bit wider than Robbie. My hips twisted with each move.

"I think your girly hips are lying!" Henry yelled, setting most of the guys off in peals of laughter.

I missed one of the ladder rungs. Gritting my teeth, I pulled the puck back to pass it through again.

"Relax, Butter!" Ray-Ray yelled. "Just imagine it's some guy's ass and you'll get it right every time."

"What the hell?" I came to an abrupt stop.

"Keep going, Butter," Coach Benoit said.

"Seriously, are you listening to them?"

"I didn't hear anything," Coach Benoit said. "Keep going."

Fuming, I recollected the puck as I slowly wove through the ladder, spinning a clover through three close cones.

As I moved to the next obstacle, stick handling through a ton of pucks, I heard Durrell hum *The Phantom of the Opera* theme. My blood went cold. I skated up hard to the net. There were four targets in each corner. As I shot, I kept hitting the crossbar. At my seventh attempt, I felt the splinter and lightness as my stick cracked.

"If you can't perform out here, how can you perform at all?" Durrell's voice rang.

I whirled on Durrell, my broken stick in hand. "What the hell's your problem?"

"I don't have a problem."

"Yes. You do. You've been treating me like crap ever since you started going out with Heather."

"Personal drama off the ice, Butter," Coach said. "Go get a new stick and finish up."

"Aren't you going to do something?"

"Here," Robbie said quickly, skating up to me. He pressed

his stick in my hand. It felt warm. Way better than mine. With the extra curve in the blade, I got all targets in nine tries.

"Thanks," I said as I handed it back to Robbie.

"Careful, Robbie," Henry said. "You might get gay germs off it."

My face heated. My fists clenched. Something inside me splintered and snapped, just like my stick had.

"Just ignore it," Robbie said beneath his breath.

To my surprise, I answered with, "No."

I pulled off my helmet and skated toward the locker room.

"Where do you think you're going?" Coach Benoit asked.

"I quit!" I yelled over my shoulder.

My teammates' eyes burned into my back as I stepped off the ice and pulled on my skate guards. Not a single person spoke. No one came after me. Not to say they were sorry, or that I should stay and gut it out.

None of the guys wanted me there. Not even Coach.

I showered slowly then packed up my bag. With a heavy sigh, I left the locker room for the last time.

DAD COULDN'T look me in the eye. He tried several times as we sat around the dinner table eating pasta and chicken, mouth opening then closing, sighing again and again. I couldn't touch my food with Dad looking at me like I broke his heart. I almost regretted my decision.

"We'll get you playing somewhere," Dad finally said, although it lacked conviction. "Some other school. Or club. Or worst case, get you in sports management."

I hung my head. My fingers knitted together. "I'm done, Dad. I don't want to do this anymore."

Dad was on his feet so quickly I didn't see him move. His

knuckles blanched from his grip on the table edge. "You're giving up because of what your teammates said? Some stupid hazing? You know what would happen if you were in the NHL? You know what fans would be saying about you?"

"It's not about what they're saying," I said, even though that wasn't entirely true. A few times I'd wondered if I was gay. I never looked at guys, but I never really had a girlfriend. I loved musicals, and musical theatre was pretty dominated by gay men. Deep down, I knew I wasn't. I could look at a man and find him attractive, in the platonic sense; I could admit, "he's a good looking guy," but I didn't get butterflies the way I would around Heather.

"What would you even do without hockey? Have you thought about that?"

I lifted my head. Maybe this was my chance. My opportunity to get what I wanted.

"I want to be an actor," I blurted.

Everything was silent around me.

"After what your brother did, you *still* want to act?" Mom said, almost snorting. "You're going to quit hockey so you can act? You know what people will think about you?"

"I don't care."

"Really? Really, you're not going to care at all that they'll think you're queer?"

"Maybe I am," I challenged.

"That's not funny."

"No, it's not funny because it's stupid as hell."

"What's gotten into you?"

"You mean me getting a backbone?"

I got up and stomped up the steps, slowing near the top, wondering if Robbie or Dad would defend me. But Robbie remained silent and Dad only said, "He was out of line."

Mom's voice sighed. "I don't know what's gotten into him."

I sat on the top of the steps to listen.

"Has he always wanted to act?" Dad murmured.

I pleaded for Robbie to say something. To be my savior and say yes. But Robbie was silent.

"It's a phase," Mom said, trying to comfort him. "I'd almost count on it. Probably he's getting affected because of the draft."

"You're probably right," Dad said with a sigh. "I don't know if I should start making calls now or later. Surely someone would give him a job as an equipment manager or something."

"You can't be too surprised. We've known since he was eight."

"I hoped he'd catch up," Dad said.

"So, we'll have him be Robbie's personal assistant. He can manage him directly."

What?

I stormed to Robbie's room, opened the door, then slammed it shut, hoping my parents would realize I overheard them.

Robbie's personal assistant? My parents degraded me to being his *personal assistant?*

I flopped on my mattress face down. I wouldn't do it. I put up with a lot but that was too much.

So I wouldn't.

There was something strangely calming in quitting hockey—the simple freedom of doing what *I* wanted. I wouldn't play hockey, I wouldn't be Robbie's assistant, and I *would* star in a musical. Soon, I'd be out of there. Off to some college on a scholarship, get a job to cover housing. Change my name, maybe even legally. I would never act under the name Betterby. In playbills, I wouldn't thank my parents.

I didn't hear Robbie enter the room but I noticed when he sat on the mattress next to mine. "I'm sorry," he said.

"Why didn't you stand up for me?" I asked.

"You know why."

"No. I don't." I sat upright. "Seriously, what's with all the cryptic stuff? Just tell me what's going on."

"I can't."

"Why not?"

Robbie got on his feet and walked to the door. "I'm getting a shower."

"You already had one."

"So you're monitoring me now?"

"Pot calling the kettle black?"

"Whatever," he said, stepping into the hallway.

I snorted and flopped on my back. "Whatever," I muttered to the empty room.

17

I don't think I'd ever slept better in my life. Being free from hockey was a relief. I wouldn't be compared to Robbie. I could focus on my acting and actually have the time to take the *pro bono* lessons. For the first time, I was an individual. Not nameless, disappearing on the ice, a replaceable player.

My stomach did a flip as I pulled into the parking lot and watched the students walking in and out of Briar Rose's front doors. Things would change today. I wasn't a hockey player; I was an actor, one in the musical, one who had an insanely hard tap routine to learn within a few months.

I turned the ignition off, locked my car behind me, and walked into the building. Everyone stared at me. Not just a few looks in the hallway. Literally *everyone* was watching me. I fought to keep from vomiting as I walked down the hall toward my locker. Word got around fast. I wasn't Robbie's winger anymore. I was an individual, standing on my own feet.

And it was terrifying.

When I turned around the corner, a large crowd had formed in a semi-circle around my locker. They parted like a corridor as I approached. I heard my name through whispers of white noise and giggles.

I weaved between them until I stood dead center and froze. The top of my locker to the bottom was covered with paper and pictures. Not just any papers and pictures, but of musicals. Musicals I'd never intended for anyone to discover I liked. *Mary Poppins, The Lion King, Shrek, Seussical the Musical, Annie Get Your Gun, Legally Blonde, Starlight Express, The Secret Garden, Cats.*

Worse than that were pages of fanfic I wrote. I picked off one of the papers and looked at it. Silenced1 was circled in red, an arrow pointing to it that read TRISTAN. GlitterB0mb was scratched out in black, permanent marker so it wasn't visible.

Everyone around me began to laugh. Or maybe they were already laughing, and I only realized it at that moment. Like I was in a void—just me and the incriminating papers—and that void dissipated into reality: I was at school, and people were laughing at me.

Although pointless, I ripped down as many papers as I could and crumpled them together. The only people who knew about me liking musicals *and* writing fan-fiction were the theatre people and Robbie, sort of. My heartbeat quickened. Maybe Robbie staged an elaborate prank. He would have done shit like this a year ago. Would have thought it was hilarious. I doubted Robbie even knew the names of most of these musicals, but nixing Robbie left Heather, and it couldn't have been Heather. She was ignoring me, but she would never go out of her way to be that cruel. She had nothing to gain from my downfall.

With papers in hand like a bouquet of weeds, I opened my locker. The inside was stuffed with printouts, pictures, and children's activity books that tumbled to the floor. I stared at the mess. There was only one person besides me who knew my locker combination.

Heather.

On the inside of the locker door, someone wrote in

permanent marker: *GROW UP TRISTAN!* Underneath that, an underlined word: FAGGOT.

I didn't recognize the handwriting.

I scooped the papers together in my arms and threw them in the garbage can. I thought about rebutting, about yelling at the voyeuristic students to knock it off, or claim that I was set up, but that wouldn't make a difference. The damage was done. Irreversible. No one forgot anything in high school. Teachers and parents always talked about people forgetting with time, but they didn't. Once a person became a target, they were a target for life. Years would pass, and I'd graduate with a bunch of "kiddie musicals" on my back.

My thoughts collided like cars on the New Jersey Turnpike at rush hour in a blizzard. I wanted to vanish like I'd never existed. More than that, I wanted to erase all my years of friendship with Heather. If it weren't for her, I probably never would have even gotten into musicals in the first place, or written fan-fiction, which was what *really* embarrassed me. Guys didn't really write fanfic. At least none I knew about. Maybe, instead of fan-fiction, I'd have spent more time on my original stories, or maybe I would have been content with hockey. I could stop listening to musical soundtracks altogether and beg to rejoin the hockey team again and be a healthy scratch the rest of the season. I could pretend that I'd had a psychotic breakdown, and Coach Benoit would say he understood. I could go to college for sports management. Or why even bother with college if I'd just be Robbie's personal assistant, living off his charity?

No. I couldn't do that. If Robbie wasn't even hospitalized after his second attempt, no way would I be able to pull the crazy card.

Even if I returned to hockey, I'd still be teased. Bullies

never let things go. Nor did the people who wanted to be friends with bullies. No one ever let things go until someone died. Then the bullies were magically the recently deceased's best friends. *I'm going to miss him so much. He was like a brother to me. We were just joking, you know?*

Because everyone always joked when it was all over. No one wanted to accept responsibility, accept the blame when things became permanent, irreversible.

Suicide.

18

By the time I got to Acting, barely anyone looked at me except Keisha. Her eyes were sympathetic, but she remained silent. I stopped in front of Heather's chair. She was texting on her phone.

"I didn't do it," she said, not even looking up.

"You're the only person who knows my locker combination."

"No, I'm not."

"Yes, you are—" I stopped myself. Then I took a step back. "Did you give my combination to Durrell?"

"They were just messing with you. It's just a prank."

"It's more than a prank, and you know it."

I turned my back to Heather and sat on the other side of the room. Durrell orchestrated this? Maybe he and Heather were together, but that didn't explain why I was a target. I'd never been a threat to their relationship.

Craig sat next to me, sheet music in hand. "Are you all right?" When I didn't answer immediately, he lowered his voice, "Want me to talk to Heather?"

"No."

He gave a sympathetic smile and extended the sheet music. "Elisa's not in. Booked a role in *Orange Is The New Black*. Some high school flashback. Soooooo . . . I need a partner. Mind going over this with me if you've got a moment?"

I took the sheet music from him. It was the "I Am Aldopho" song. "You want me to be the Chaperone?" I asked, unable to keep an amused smirk off my face. "Wouldn't you want to choose someone like Keisha instead?"

"Gorgeous as she is, I'd rather pretend to seduce someone with rippling abs," Craig said, throwing a hand over his heart. But then, he became more serious again. "You sure you don't want me to talk to Heather? I mean, it's even making *me* uncomfortable. You two were supposed to be like conjoined."

"It's fine."

"You sure?" Craig asked. "I just don't want you to get hurt."

"A little late for that."

"Well, more hurt than you already are. Seriously, you're one of my besties, even though you're, you know, straight." He paused, over-dramatically leaning toward me, wiggling his eyebrows. "Then again, maybe that's why I'm so unusually attracted to you."

I snorted, "You are not."

"You're right. I'm not. Your twin's the hot one."

"Craig!"

We burst out laughing. I pulled Craig into a headlock as he made kissy faces at me and tried to wrestle me to the ground. Ms. Price interrupted us, "Are you two rehearsing? Because the words out of your mouths don't sound like they're from *The Drowsy Chaperone*."

Despite the shitty morning, I brightly said, "Would you believe us if we said it was an interpretive ballet of *The Drowsy Chaperone*?"

"Crossed over with *The Book of Mormon*," Craig joined me.

"But politically correct! Sort of. Only not really."

"Complete with a WWE brawl, which we'd be more than happy to demonstrate."

"But we'll need a lot of props first, and a good fight captain. Anyone here know *tai kwon do?*"

Although Ms. Price laughed, Heather's voice filtered through the commotion, a voice only I was meant to hear. "Maybe if you learned how to dance half as good as Craig, people would take you more seriously."

I stopped laughing.

"What's wrong?" Craig asked.

"Nothing," I mumbled. I stared at the sheet music just so I wouldn't have to look anyone in the eye.

Heather was right. I'd never be taken seriously. I was a senior. Learning choreography from Heather and Youtube videos wasn't enough to make up for such a late start. Those guys at the audition were just being nice. She was probably right—I was cast as Robert because I could skate. Hell, if Robbie auditioned, he probably would have been cast as Robert before me.

By the end of class, I'd gone through "I Am Aldolpho" twice with Craig and had sweat through my spare T-shirt as learning the tap choreography for "Cold Feets" in a pair of borrowed shoes, which would be my biggest number. I was so exhausted I almost forgot what would face me once I left the sanctuary of class. But it came back to me fast the moment I was shoved against a locker hard enough to knock the breath out of me.

19

My sides ached from people shoving into me any time I walked down the hall. Someone tried to trip me on the stairs. I barely caught the railing in time. I continued to the cafeteria, stopping outside its doors and wondered whether it was worth it.

Hesitantly, I entered the cafeteria. I wanted a hot lunch, but I grabbed a yogurt, small bag of Fritos, and a bottle of V8 so I could avoid the line. I passed Heather on the way to our old table. Durrell and the guys didn't even look at me. I thought I heard Keisha say my name, but when I turned my head she was staring at her lunch tray.

As soon as I sat down, I was pelted with crumpled paper balls. Noticing a little bit of pencil on the lined paper, I opened one up—*MUSICAL FAG*. Then another—*R U A PEDO IF U LIKE ANNIE?*

I shrank down in my seat like I could fold myself and disappear. Maybe it was time to start taking a paper bag lunch to school and seeing if I could eat in the music room with the band geeks. Even though Craig and his self-dubbed Gay-Bros were fun in acting, I couldn't sit with them. Not unless I wanted to get the shit kicked out of me.

I finished my yogurt and was just about to open the bag of Fritos, when I noticed some of the football jocks across the cafeteria. Several of them glanced in my direction, then they got up and walked toward me. Durrell wrapped his arm around Heather's shoulder and pointed at me. Heather looked me dead in the eye, smirked, and kissed Durrell.

The football jocks came closer. I shoved the bag of Fritos and the bottle of V8 into my backpack so I could make a getaway.

"Relax," one of the guys, Eric, said. His smirk was the cruelest. I picked up my backpack anyway and stood to leave, but he forced me back down. "No, stay."

I looked at the exit. Could I outrun them? Possibly, but that would only make things worse the next time.

I looked around the football jocks to the Gay-Bros' table. Craig and I made eye contact. I mouthed a plea for help. But Craig shook his head apologetically and looked away. Just like everyone else at the table.

I looked toward Durrell's table, tried to make eye contact with my former teammates. They refused to look at me either. But Heather stared at me dead on. Beside her, an empty chair where Keisha normally sat.

"Why don't you dance? Do some of that gay ballet stuff," Eric taunted.

"I don't do ballet," I lied.

"Or do you just dance alone in your bedroom when you think no one's watching?"

I thought about Heather, about rehearsing with her. I thought about the Youtube barre exercises I practiced. How the hell did they know about that?

Eric's hand closed on the back of my neck, gripping tightly enough for it to hurt.

"You know what's going to happen next," Eric said quietly. He was right; I knew what was coming. I clenched my fists.

I'd never been in a single hockey fight, and now I was to go against football players who towered over me. In the corner of my eye, I saw people pull out their cellphones to take video. A lunch aid slipped into the hallway.

I braced my body and swung my fist out. I barely caught his side before Eric's friends forced my arms behind my back. I tried to kick free, back arching as Eric took a swing. The harsh pain of knuckles collided into my stomach. His class ring dug deep in my side. I gasped for breath, my body wriggling to break free.

With a knee to my back, they forced me to the ground, slamming my face against the floor. A boot connected with my ribs moments before I was flipped on my back. Eric held a banana in front of my face. "Suck it, musical fag." I turned my head to the side, teeth grit, trying not to cry. "Suck it like a dick!"

"Leave my brother alone."

The pressure around me eased. I was freed. I scrambled to my feet, gripping a chair for support as the cafeteria spun.

Robbie stood at the end of the table, hands balled up in fists. His hateful glare was locked on Eric. He might have been shorter than Eric and the football guys, but he made them look small, carrying himself large. His elbows bent out, muscle definition clear. He'd be faster than the football guys, more wiry and quick on his feet. Football guys might have known how to tackle, but hockey guys *fought*. They policed the ice, righting wrongs. I was being wronged, and Robbie rarely lost a fight.

Behind Robbie, at his table, I saw Raiden stand up, prepared to jump in if things got out of hand.

The football guys almost shrank back. I had never seen Robbie look so dangerous. He never looked this scary when he was on the ice. His fake lip ring made him look more intimidating, and his bleached blond hair made his brown eyes even darker. Like they were black, fiery coal or molten lava.

"We were just joking around," Eric tried to explain, still trying to laugh, to smile, to say anything to pacify Robbie.

"Didn't look like joking to me." Robbie took a step closer. "Tristan, you okay?"

I couldn't even wheeze an answer. Robbie stepped up to me and gently pressed on my shoulder until I eased myself on the chair

Eric tried to laugh again, each guffaw breaking up his nervousness. "It was just a joke. Chill. I mean, you used to haze him all the time."

"I never made him try to choke."

Eric swallowed. "I mean, you have to admit that listening to musicals is a faggy thing to do."

"I don't have to admit *anything.*"

I sank deeper into my chair, completely limp, hurting, and mute from fear. Robbie's face contorted the same way it always did when he was figuring out what to say. "Some straight guys like musicals. And some gay guys—" Robbie's voice cut off. There was something I couldn't place in his expression. Like he was going to throw up, or scream, or something.

"Some gay guys," he repeated.

My brother shifted his weight. He was breathing fast and heavily. He was trying to stand tall, to look intimidating, but I could sense his fear. While seconds ago, he gave the appearance of towering, now he looked small. So small.

Robbie said, "Some gay guys play hockey."

My chest restricted harder than when I was punched. I stared at my brother. Everything became startlingly clear. How many times had Robbie talked with me, saying, "they don't know," again and again and again? Robbie's pleas in the kitchen with the knife. My intestines twisted into knots, hurting more than the bruises that would form.

Eric laughed. "What? You're saying all these fags are wanting to play hockey in pink jerseys?"

"Oh, because being gay means pink and sparkles and unicorns. Yeah, real mature, Eric," Robbie snapped.

"Jesus, Robbie. Chill. It's not like you're some homo," Eric said defensively, holding up his hands.

Robbie's eyes narrowed into thinner slits. My throat tightened. Robbie wasn't considering doing here and now what I feared . . . could he? Not in front of everyone, just to protect me?

"Robbie," I finally whispered. He broke his glare to look at me. Maybe we weren't super close, but I couldn't let him do this. I wasn't worth him losing his future. More than his favorite sport, his life. "Don't."

I thought he might have faltered. There was a sheen over his dark eyes. I extended my hand toward him, but he didn't reach for me.

Instead, Robbie turned his full attention to Eric. I gripped onto the bottom of my seat. Felt dried chewing gum brush against my knuckle.

Robbie leaned toward Eric. His voice lowered in pitch. "Actually, I am."

And then, in an even deeper growl, Robbie said, "Get the hell away from my brother before I break your fucking jaw."

There was a dead silence throughout the cafeteria. Hundreds of eyes and cellphones were fixed on our table. On Robbie.

Eric looked stunned, opening and closing his mouth a few times before he turned his back to the table. Some of the hockey guys stared wide-eyed. Durrell's face turned a sickly color, the pallor of guilt. Raiden left the cafeteria in a hurry. I swore I saw Heather smile.

Robbie continued glaring at Eric until he was across the cafeteria, even mouthing, "I will break you," when it looked like Eric might return. Only when Eric was far enough away did Robbie drop into the chair directly across from me. He rested his face in his hands. "Damn it."

"You didn't have to do that," I said, trembling slightly.

He didn't look at me. "Yeah, I did."

"But your career—"

"Yeah," he said, barely audible. "I know."

Desperately, I tried to make eye contact with my twin. I reached out across the table to touch his arm, but he yanked it away from me. The bell signaled the end of lunch. Robbie got to his feet and slung his backpack over his shoulder.

"I'll see you after practice." He started to the cafeteria exit then paused. "If anyone, and I mean *anyone*, gives you crap, promise to tell me?"

"But—"

"Promise me, Tristan. Right now. Or I swear to God, I will make you get dentures."

Firm. Non-negotiable.

I nodded. Robbie looked relieved and continued out of the cafeteria. My mind was reeling. My twin outed himself in front of the entire school just to protect me.

Me.

And it worked.

For the rest of the day, people left me alone. No papers were thrown at me, no taunts about musicals and needing to grow up. People barely even acknowledged me. Just like before. All at once, it didn't matter that my former-best friend betrayed me. Now I had a closer bond with someone who mattered.

Someone I thought I barely knew, or would ever get to know. Someone who had desperately been trying to get my attention for years, and until now I completely ignored.

My brother.

My twin.

Robbie.

20

Sometimes, the Internet really sucked. Without having a face to directly confront, people typed all the stuff they wouldn't dare say in person. Cyber-bullying and trolling is unavoidable to anyone who uses the Internet. Tumblr, Facebook, Twitter, Instagram. Parents and teachers always tell bullied kids to ignore it, but they don't get that it's impossible to ignore something in your face at every turn. They're too old to understand that things now are different than when they were young and used America Online on 28.8 kb/s dial-up modems.

After we came home—me from my first rehearsal, Robbie from practice—we avoided going up to his room and using our computers. My bruises from the lunch fight starting to turn eggplant and yellow.

There were a few awkward moments of eye contact and fumbled half-starts, but we didn't really talk. I didn't tell Robbie that I was sorry; he didn't tell me how he got the cut on his face. Neither one of us wanted to see the online damage that was undoubtedly waiting for us. We cleaned the house and made dinner without complaint, then stalled in the living room. Robbie agreed to watch *Into The Woods* with me since Mom and Dad were out, although he barely paid attention. When the movie was over, he grabbed the remote and put on the game—New Jersey Devils versus Tampa Bay

Lightning—and I had to listen to him bitch after Stamkos got a power-play goal on a breakaway.

I got out *Othello* from my backpack and started to do my reading for next week. By the time the game was over and Robbie's voice was hoarse from screaming at the refs, I'd read through most of *Othello*, and wasn't in the mood to see another game when Robbie said he wanted to see what happened on the west coast.

"You sure you don't want to see it?" Robbie asked, almost pleading. "San Jose Sharks versus the Minnesota Wild."

"Not really," I admitted. Robbie looked down. I probably shouldn't have said that, especially after what he sacrificed for me, but I had to be honest. I liked hockey, but I didn't love it. Robbie didn't just love hockey; he breathed it.

I walked up to Robbie's room and sat at the table. Sooner or later, I'd need to address the inevitable. I ignored the number of notifications on my own Facebook page as I typed in my twin's name. My stomach twisted when the page loaded. Robbie's entire timeline was filled with questions and comments:

> *are you really gay?*
> *did u just say that so tristan wudnt get picked on?*
> *r u a fag?*
> *What the hell was up with lunch???????*
> *call me.*
> *faggot*
> *I'll always support you, no matter who or what you are. <3*
> *we need to talk. Call me.*
> *no fags on the hockey team*
> *call me.*
> *WTF!?!??!?!?!?!?!*
> *I alaways kenw you were gya!1*

BIG HUGS
You need Jesus. I'll pray for you. It's not too late.
soap on a rope lawlz

There wasn't a single post from Raiden, which was weird since he always spammed Robbie's Facebook with Imgur memes and Youtube videos.

Even though none of those messages were directed at me, I felt hollow.

My own Facebook was getting bombarded with comments, too, though not on the same scale. There was a sweet one from Keisha: *Just wanted to send hugs to you and Robbie and say hang in there. Tell him I said yay for gay! =)* Maybe it was just in my head, but lately it seemed like she had been going out of her way to talk to me.

Other students posted links to musical parody videos on Youtube that were pretty funny, like "If You Were Gay" from *Avenue Q,* but some of the others weren't so great. I deleted all of the comments that made fun of me for liking "kiddie musicals," and deleted the ones that made fun of me with the straight twin/gay twin crap, but for each one I deleted, it seemed like three more would appear, some even with a hashtag #freedomofspeech, #nohomo, or a super offensive "no offense but." I wondered if I should have been deleting people from Facebook rather than deleting comments, but I didn't want to seem unpopular. Facebook friends showed social hierarchy. No one took anybody seriously if they had under four hundred friends. Even three hundred and ninety-nine friends wasn't good enough.

I quickly typed a status: *My brother is the bravest person I know.*

I waited a moment before deleting what I typed without posting it.

"How bad is it?" Robbie asked from the doorway holding an

ice pack. I hadn't even heard him come up the stairs. Before I had the chance to answer, Robbie rubbed his forehead and said, "Never mind. I'll see for myself."

"Don't," I said, surprised I found my voice. "Give me your password and I'll take care of it."

Robbie hesitated and rubbed his hands together. "They'll say I'm a pussy if you delete posts."

"They're going to say stuff anyway."

Robbie sighed. I thought he might tell me off, but instead he said, "Margarine sixteen. No space. Lowercase. For my password, I mean." He sat on his mattress and flipped through his phone.

I typed in *margarine16* and my throat tightened.

There were hundreds of notifications and private messages. I started with his timeline, changing the setting so that only Robbie would be able to post on it. Then I deleted every single hostile post, leaving up the few ones of support, pressing the "Like" button on those. Like Keisha—who already left a note on my Facebook—who wrote: *You should check out something like You Can Play or It Gets Better. I can help you if you want.*

I moved to the private messages next.

One from Durrell immediately popped up.

Dude, I'm so sorry. I wouldn't have said that crap about T if I knew. No promises but I'll try to get the guys to back off you, aiight? Be strong, bro.

I frowned. *That* was the Durrell I know. The one who was so cool. Not the monster who hazed me after stealing my best friend. Although I shouldn't have, I scrolled up through the message to see if there was anything else about me. There wasn't. They talked about hockey, plans, scouts, college versus juniors, and sometimes a few directions to parties.

Behind me, I heard Robbie hurl his phone at his mattress.

I turned around on the computer chair. "Raiden," he said, answering my unspoken question.

"What'd he say?"

"Nothing. Literally," he mumbled. "Won't return any of my texts." He got to his feet. "I'm taking a shower."

I waited for Robbie to leave the room before I scrolled through his Facebook inbox. It wasn't hard to find a convo with Raiden.

Robbie: What up beauty? ;)
Raiden: omg think im still drnk hahahaa
Robbie: LOL!! Yeah, me too. I dunno about you but no regrets here. ;)
Raiden: huh? y regrets when we were waisted?
Robbie: . . . oh. Yeah. i guess that was stupid of me to write.

Robbie's text deteriorated with each message. I read everything, scrolling through Imgur memes and Youtube videos until a new message at the bottom popped up, written in perfect text:

Raiden: I deserved to know.

Even though it was hard to let things be, I made myself log out of Robbie's Facebook after one last glance. I couldn't prevent future messages, but at least his wall would be spared. Then I went into Word so I could try to write something. I only gazed at the unfinished dolphin story. I couldn't concentrate. By the time Robbie returned from a shower, I hoped the worst would be gone. Especially as he logged on to his computer.

Periodically, I'd glance at Robbie's computer wondering what he was doing, or how much worse his Facebook page had become since he came out. But Robbie wasn't in Facebook. He was in some chat room.

"Do you mind?" Robbie said, not looking away from his screen. Embarrassed at being caught, I looked away from his monitor, but not for long.

When Robbie got up to go to the bathroom, I leaned sideways to look at his screen. He was in a chat room for depression. A private window was centered on the screen. I knew I shouldn't, but I was curious about what my brother was doing to cope. I scrolled to the top of the conversation and began to read.

Jimmy2416: hey wanna chat?
hockeylover15: Sure. ASL or something, right?
Jimmy2415: LOL do people still ask that?
hockeylover15: No idea. I haven't used IM in years.
Jimmy2416: LOL ok 24/m/pa you?
hockeylover15: 18/M/NJ
Jimmy2416: ur profile says ur 15
Jimmy2416: ?
hockeylover15: Oh yeah. That's when I made my account. Guess I haven't updated in awhile.
Jimmy2416: riiiight. u in high school or college then?
hockeylover15: High school. I'm a senior.
Jimmy2416: cool
Jimmy2416: gotta pic?

I felt breath by my ear and turned around. Robbie glowered over me. "Uh . . . sorry," I mumbled and moved back to my computer. "I didn't see that much. Honest."

"You shouldn't have seen anything," he said bitterly.

"I'm sorry." I rubbed the back of my neck. "So, what's up with the depressed chat room?"

Robbie put his headphones on and blasted Robyn.

Translation: Screw you.

I kind of deserved that.

"Hey Robbie?" He didn't hear me. I cleared my throat and more loudly said, "Robbie?"

"*What?*" He snapped as he pulled them off. Now, Ani DiFranco blasted through his headphones. If he was listening to her, he was definitely angry. I shrank back in my seat as Robbie glowered at me. I was pushing it too far. I knew I was. He made a huge sacrifice for me, and I couldn't leave it alone. Like scratching at a scab.

I braced myself for a punch and stammered, "What do you think's going to happen at school on Monday?"

Robbie looked at the computer again. He rubbed the back of his neck, then scratched through his bleached hair, more subdued. "You probably don't have to worry. Straight dude who likes musicals is a lot less interesting than the gay hockey prospect."

I felt awful for Robbie, and wanted to talk to him more, or something, but I said nothing. Speaking would cheapen that sacrifice. Whatever I said would never be able to equal the kindness he gave me at lunch. I saw Robbie glance at me from the corner of his eye, like he was waiting, hoping, praying, that I'd say something, but I was still mute. I couldn't give him what he wanted. I didn't know how.

Robbie needed help. Robbie was alone, and was pleading for help. And maybe he was pleading for help from me. Or maybe that was me just hoping he was. Wishing that maybe, somehow, through this mess, someone would think I was important, or worth getting to know. That maybe the favorite son would realize the forgotten son was a decent guy. That someone was actually grateful for me.

But that wouldn't ever happen. Not when I couldn't defend myself against a bully and had nothing to offer my brother in exchange for his sacrifice. He wouldn't be grateful because there was nothing to be grateful for. I would continue to live in his shadow, a disgrace.

21

On Monday morning before homeroom, Eric's group approached. I turned to my locker and watched them out of the corner of my eye. Eric's fists were balled. Praying they would pass me, I continued turning the lock. I had to pretend I wasn't scared or else whatever beating I was bound to get would be multiplied.

There was a *clang-bam-bang*, the sound of a body colliding with metal. I turned. Robbie was pinned by Eric. Robbie used his tongue to play with his fake lip piercing, turning the ball on the end of the ring around.

"Heh," he said with a smirk, lips curling up. "That all you got, bitch?"

In that moment, I was convinced that Robbie was insane and I'd be peeling him off the ground. Yet, Eric released his shoulders abruptly and shoved past him muttering, "Homo." Further down the hall, I locked eyes with Durrell for a moment before he turned away.

"You okay?" I ventured to ask my brother.

Robbie didn't answer. He watched them walk away and rubbed his shoulder with his knuckles. His middle finger raised.

"Robbie?" I tried again.

But Robbie was gazing into the distance the same way I

did when I got lost in musicals and short stories. Maybe he just didn't hear me. Finally, without looking at me, he said, "I have to be."

The bell rang, and Robbie walked ahead of me to World Civilizations. I jogged to catch up with him. This was just the beginning of a long road we'd be traveling on, but Robbie didn't want a traveling companion. Robbie wanted to go solo.

I DIDN'T see Robbie in the cafeteria at lunch. There was an empty chair next to Raiden, like no one wanted to touch it. Robbie's presence was a ghost.

I kind of wished he was at the cafeteria. Eating alone really sucked, especially now. I spent half of lunch reading Louise Erdrich's *The Round House* before noticing something in the corner of my eye. A bit of blue jeans. I looked up. It was Keisha.

I closed my book. "Hey. What's up?"

"Nothing. I—" Keisha frowned a little. "I'm having a birthday party. Never got a sweet sixteen so I figured spectacular seventeen would do. I wanted to invite you. Robbie, too."

"You seriously want to invite us? What about Heather and Durrell and—"

"Screw them," she said. "Seriously, it's *my* party. Not theirs. And I want you both there." She paused then. "But if you think Robbie would get teased and try to, you know, hurt himself again—"

My body turned to stone. "Who told you that?"

"Heather. Why?" Keisha looked at me then put her hand on her mouth. "I wasn't supposed to know, was I?"

"No one's supposed to know." My fingers curled over my knees. "If it affects his *draftability*, my parents will literally kill me. *Literally.* God, he'd probably actually go through with it if he didn't get drafted. Shit."

Keisha looked at the ground. The whites in her eyes glistened. My stomach ached. I didn't want to make her cry. "I didn't mean to yell. I just . . . Robbie's given up so much for me."

"I shouldn't have said anything. I'm sorry. I just—I just wanted you to come to my party. And Robbie, too, of course. I mean, I don't know. I'm sorry. I probably shouldn't have said anything."

I didn't know how to reply, or how I was supposed to feel. Keisha probably would get ripped on just for talking to me, even in passing, or standing at my table twisting her thick hair like she didn't know whether she was breaking some unspoken rule—never talk with a friend's former friend.

"I want to go," I said gently and looked Keisha in the eyes. I squeezed her hand, looked at her chipped, purple nail polish. "I wasn't supposed to tell anyone this, but my parents want me to monitor Robbie at all times. If I can talk him into going, we'll be there. I'm not sure I can, but I'll try."

"I hope you can." She looked over her shoulder and pulled her hand away abruptly. "I need to go."

Hurriedly, Keisha scooted back to Durrell's table and sat next to Heather. Heather turned to her and said something that made Keisha wilt. My fists clenched under the table.

I thought about Keisha, and her fears of being rejected by her friends. Fears of becoming an outcast, just like my twin. Keisha lacked courage, but was kind. She didn't belong in that group. She didn't belong with Heather.

After finishing my homework that evening, I went through her Facebook. I read her interests section. She liked horses, *Harry Potter,* and astronomy. I thought for a long time about what I could buy her, but she probably was the type who bought anything she'd want. Material possessions wouldn't mean that much to her. Handmade, though . . .

I pulled up Word. It was hard to ignore the unfinished story about the dolphin people. That was the wrong sort of story to give her. I needed to make something special. Something with fluff. I began to write:

It was late August when Sagittarius leapt from the skies to Earth. When standing in the clouds, he noticed a girl on land. She sat on a rock near a waterfall, playing a pan flute. The music was intoxicating. Sagittarius had thought he had loved once before, but the lady centaurs never had a song with that much emotion, or that much beauty.

Fearlessly, Sagittarius landed near the woman. He opened his mouth to speak, but the woman was terrified of his half-human, half-horse body. "Please, don't be frightened," he begged. "I came from the skies because you are the most beautiful woman I have ever seen. I'm in love with you."

"But you can't be."

"But I am."

"But how could I love half a man?"

Crushed, Sagittarius galloped away, head bowed down in shame, trying to tune out the sound of her voice crying, "Wait! Please, come back."

But he didn't turn back. He became ashamed, ashamed of the creature he was. No. The woman could not love a beast. She was too divine.

Sagittarius dipped his fingers into the trickle of a creek and withdrew a sword made of water, slicing the blade through his body.

Cut in two, he now was freed from his body. The human half used his arms to crawl on the ground, delighted that now he wasn't a creature, a beast, but although he had his mind, he no longer had his heart. His heart was in the horse half, a headless body that galloped over the hills, down ravines, unable to whinny, unable to do anything but obey his heart's desire and run.

It took ten days for the woman with her flute to find Sagittarius's human half on the ground, a trail of dried blood behind him. She turned him over and looked at his broken face. "Will you love me now, even if I have no heart?" he asked, but his voice lacked emotion.

The woman began to weep, grieved, wishing to undo her harsh words, for now this half-man—all human—had no heart, no emotion, nothing but the memory of being in love and needing to remain in love. She lifted Sagittarius' emotionless torso and carried him across the Earth, trying to find the rest of his body. To find his heart, his feelings, his love.

Finally, they saw the body lying down. Without a mind, the horse body ran itself to the point of breaking all four of his legs, quivering, belly rising and falling in shakes. Without a heart, Sagittarius had no sympathy for his other self—find me another body, then I can love you properly.

But the girl had to remedy this. She cried as she placed the bodies together, sewing their skins together with thread from the long grasses. When she tied the last knot, Sagittarius started to weep, for with a heart, he felt pain at his broken body, his suffering legs that now were unable to move.

"I do love you," the girl said, handing him her flute as they kissed. The magic of their kiss formed a gateway to the skies, and without

gravity holding him down, Sagittarius lifted into the sky. The girl held onto his tail as long as she could until the hairs snapped and she fell to the ground, crashing into the Earth, and became a waterfall.

I printed out the story and had to dog-ear the pages since our stapler was gone. I'm not sure what my parents thought Robbie would do with a stapler, and didn't ask either. At the top, I wrote, "Happy birthday, Keisha," with a smiley face and signed with nothing special—just a dash and my name, *Tristan.* Boring, plain. Nothing memorable. But this wasn't about being memorable. This was about a gift for someone who was kind. Someone who was a friend.

I folded up the story in an envelope, licked it shut, and doodled a little birthday cake on the front. Then I put the letter in my backpack. I'd give it to her tomorrow, or slip it in her locker if I didn't see her. I hoped she'd like it.

22

It took me a little more than a week to have the balls to slip the story through the vents in Keisha's locker. Thinking about her was a welcome mental break from worrying about my brother, which was exhausting. But after slipping it in her locker, I cycled through feelings of worry and self-loathing, trembling through the first half of World Civilizations IV. It took a while for me to question whether maybe it wasn't me that was shaking, but Robbie, sitting in front of me. Mr. Tan left the room and someone coughed, "Fudge packer!" Robbie turned his head. The expression on his face was nothing I'd ever seen before, a sort of anguish I didn't know existed. I tapped the back of his shoulder and said, "They're baiting you."

Robbie didn't budge for several moments. Then he turned in his seat and looked at me. "I don't know how long I can do this anymore."

"Do what anymore?"

Robbie bit his lip, tugging his fake piercing inside his mouth. Then he turned his back to me. His shoulders quivered, like he was waiting for something to happen. An unknown horror he couldn't share, that only Robbie could feel, could see. I needed to ask him about that, hound him about what was wrong, ask Mr. Tan if we could take a moment when he came back in the classroom, but I couldn't. I didn't know how.

Maybe I could talk with him at lunch, giving myself a little extra time to figure out the right words to say. A few more hours until I was in a better mindset to deal with whatever answer I would receive.

At lunch, Robbie was sitting at my table, not eating. "Aren't you supposed to be gaining weight?" I asked as I set down my tray across from him.

"What's the point?" Robbie mumbled. "I'm not going to get drafted."

"Oh, come on. They're not going to ignore you just because you're gay."

"Just wait. You'll see."

"By the way," I began, "earlier you said something that kind of worried—"

"Hey, Tristan!"

Both my brother and I turned to the sound. It was Keisha. She wove through the tables to get to me, hair pulled up in a curlhawk.

"Hey, Keisha. What's up?" I tried to look calm and cool even though I wanted to run and scream and do everything I could to get away. Years ago, Heather had told me my original stories weren't great. The fanfic was fine, but original stuff? Forget about it. It didn't matter that Robbie said mine was better. He didn't really read or anything. He wouldn't know.

I sucked in a breath and prepared myself for failure.

Keisha stopped in front of me. I looked at her earrings instead of her face. "I just got your story," she said, voice fast and excited. My head snapped up and I met her eyes. Did she like it?

"Story?" Robbie asked, quirking his brow.

"You seriously wrote that for me?" Keisha continued, too

excited to stop. "That was . . . that was just incredible! It was so good, seriously. You should see if you can get it published or something. It's so pretty."

Warmth spread through my body. I kept my head low to keep from blushing and bit my lip the way Robbie often did. For years, Keisha was just someone I noticed in passing, on stage, but otherwise not at all. I'm not sure how. She just blended into the background when Heather was the star.

I fumbled over my words, "Well, yeah. I mean, I wanted to do something special for your birthday. Seventeen only happens once, right? I guess I should have waited to give it to you at your party, but um—"

"Screw that! Then I wouldn't have been able to read it *today!*" She gave me a hug unexpectedly. "That's like seriously the sweetest thing a guy's ever done for me!" I stood awkwardly before I embraced her in return, not sure whether I should hug back with one arm or two, or how snug I should squeeze her, or where I should even put my hands since she was taller than Heather. I didn't want to seem disinterested, but I didn't want to seem clingy or creepy or accidentally grab her ass either.

Over her shoulder, Robbie made a kissy-face gesture. But rather than nasty mocking, he was beaming. Like he was ecstatic for me. For a few seconds, I could forget he was depressed.

She finally pulled back, happy, and maybe a little embarrassed, like me. "Just . . . thank you."

"I'm uh. I'm glad you like it, Keisha. Really."

She shifted her weight from foot to foot. "So hey, I was wondering . . . do you want to sit with us for lunch today? Robbie, too, of course," she added quickly as an afterthought.

Robbie shook his head and got to his feet. "Nah, you guys can go suck face on your own. I've got stuff to do."

"Robbie!" I hissed.

Keisha laughed and blushed. "Well, I hope I'll see you both at my party."

"What party?" Robbie asked.

"Tristan didn't tell you you're invited to my birthday?" Keisha asked with a hint of disappointment.

It was my moment, the chance I was waiting for. I knew it was sort of wrong and self-serving, but I put Robbie on the spot. "I was going to. I just was worried he'd say no."

"Say no to what?" My brother asked.

Hook. Line. Sinker.

Maybe my brother would say no to me, but I was certain that anyone would have a hard time telling Keisha no. She was too sweet.

"I'm having a party for my birthday at the old cinema," Keisha said. "I'd really love it if you and Tristan came. I mean, I know it's been really rough for you, but it'd mean a lot, you know?"

My brother became stock still, freezing the way I often did when I was put on the spot. And, for a moment, I felt absolutely horrible.

"You don't need to if it's too much," I said quietly.

My words seemed to snap Robbie out of it. Politely, he said, "Maybe."

"Please try to come."

"No promises." Without another word, Robbie walked out, frowning at me. Like he was disappointed in me. I was disappointed in me, too.

Keisha smiled at me. "Come on, Tristan. Come eat with us, please."

"Won't they mind?" I asked, not feeling quite as enthused as I did a few minutes ago.

"Probably, but I don't care. You're my friend."

I picked up my tray and followed Keisha to the table. Heather and Durrell looked surprised to see me, and more surprised when Keisha pulled up a chair at the end of the table next to her.

I ate lunch relatively quietly, listened to everyone else talk, nodded my head accordingly, and kept smiling. The more I smiled, the more Heather seemed to hurt. She squirmed in her seat, looking quickly between Durrell and me, an uncertainty on her face. I grinned in return. Being happy with her friends was my best weapon. I didn't even need to say anything nasty or be a jerk, just show Heather that I could live without her in my life. Besides, I liked joking around with Keisha. She was really smart and really funny. She was also really pretty with her dark skin and even darker hair with its constantly changing style. Even though I wrote her a short story, maybe I'd get her earrings for her birthday. It'd look great with the curlhawk.

The rest of the day I was smiling, thinking about lunch, thinking about Keisha more as I thought about Robbie less. I started feeling optimistic. Things were finally going right. Things were finally going better than just back to normal.

AT THE end of the day, Robbie was waiting at my locker. "So, about Keisha's party . . ."

"It's Saturday," I said, "I know it's a lot to ask, but I need you to go. Dad and Mom'll flip out if I try to go without you."

"It's right after a game. Matinee, remember?"

"Do you need to go out with the guys afterward?" I asked hesitantly.

Robbie stalled. He pulled his fake piercing in his mouth when he bit his lip. "How much do you like Keisha?"

Truthfully, I said, "I don't know yet."

"But you think you might like her? More than a 'she's pretty and I'm horny' sort of thing?"

I thought about it for a few moments. Keisha *was* pretty. Very pretty. Her face was unique, angles making her look almost goddess-esque. The way she styled her dark brown, curly hair always complemented her personality. Fun. Sweet. Strong. And most importantly, kind.

"Yeah," I said. "I really think I do."

Robbie nodded. "Pretty sure I owe you."

"Seriously? You'll go?"

"I can be nice once in a while," Robbie said, forcing a smile that made him seem even sadder. I wanted to embrace him but I didn't trust myself not to back down, to give myself a reason to be miserable. Robbie going was a gift to me. And like hell I was going to blow it. Not this time.

23

It was weird not being on the ice for a game, and even weirder watching warm-ups. I sat next to Dad, halfway up the stands. Dad never liked sitting on the glass unless it was a championship game. Being further back allowed him to see the big picture and to watch the scouts' reactions. Mom sat on the other side of us. She hadn't said a single word to me. She also wasn't glued to her iPhone, surprisingly, fingers bunching up around the strap of her purse.

Robbie skated up to center ice for the opening face-off. We had never been the biggest guys on the ice at 5'10, but Robbie looked downright tiny. The referee dropped the puck, both centers' sticks snaked out. Robbie moved in a slight daze as the puck left his possession. He rarely lost the opening face-off. Beau barked something to him as our opponents redirected the puck and forced it into our zone. Robbie chased after them, unsteady on his skates.

"He looks terrible without you," Dad murmured.

With each shift, Robbie scrambled for the puck, head swiveling each side to find someone to pass to before he'd get trapped. He fell down with each hook and trip, all uncalled, like the refs were ignoring him. Their defenders rattled him off the puck, forcing him to dump and chase.

"Pass it to him," I said beneath my breath as Robbie skated

to the slot, the net wide open. Henry wouldn't even look at him. Robbie banged his stick against the ice, trying to draw his attention but it was no use. From afar, I heard my twin scream something but his words were unintelligible.

The first period ended. The second came and went, two goals against. The third not much different, except Beau was able to score, the puck going just below the blocker.

Only when there was less than two minutes to go did the team started passing the puck to Robbie. He tore up center ice looking almost rabid, passing the puck back toward Raiden as he looked to his right. Immediately, I felt sick. Robbie was looking for me.

He received the puck on its side, barely able to get possession. But the goalie fell for the move, skidding and leaving a wide open net. My brother's shot hit the crossbar. On the rebound, he missed the net altogether.

The end buzzer sounded. A 2-1 loss when it should have gone into overtime.

Robbie stayed on the ice a bit blankly as he looked around the stands for us. I stood up and waved, trying to draw his attention, but he skated back toward the locker room. I don't think he saw me.

"Check on your brother. I'm doing damage control," Dad said, getting up and making a beeline toward the press box. Mom surprised me as she got up and followed him. If she was interfering, then it was a lot worse than I'd thought. His draft rankings were dropping faster than the New York Stock Exchange. One bad game could make a difference from a high second, or even possibly late first rounder from a seventh, or worse.

I frowned and went down the steps, scooting along the

concourse before I slipped into the locker room. I could hear screaming before I even opened the door.

"You played like shit," Coach said.

"They wouldn't pass to me."

"Don't give me excuses. Maybe you're just some gimmick, like your brother."

I pressed against the side of the lockers, out of sight, until I saw Coach stalk out.

Then I heard another voice. Henry's. "It's God punishing you."

"Don't you dare bring God into this." Robbie's voice escalated. "I was wide open."

"Just like how the net was wide open and you missed." I was surprised. It was Raiden's voice, without question. There was something in his tone besides anger. Something I couldn't put my finger on.

"That wouldn't have been a problem if—the hell are you doing?"

There was a scuffling, then a loud shriek. Robbie's shriek. "GET OFF!"

Finally, I exploded into the locker room. It was empty. I raced to the showers just as they shoved my brother on the floor in one of the stalls, nude. Holding him as Henry turned the tap as hot as it could go. My brother's skin was red as a lobster.

I ran as fast as I could toward the group, shifting my body to hip-check Henry hard into the shower wall. Henry grunted, doubled over. "The hell is wrong with you?" I snarled, twisting the faucet off. "All of you!"

"Stay out of this, Butter," Beau said.

"Not if you're not going to protect one of your teammates. How can you call yourself captain?"

Beau's lips pulled in a taut line. "Clear out," he instructed the others, leading the pack, not offering an apology.

Robbie began to shake hard, hands clenching into fists. His face screwed up in an effort not to cry. I grabbed a towel and knelt next to my twin, ignoring the wetness that soaked through my pants, and handed it over. He pressed it to his face instead of his red body.

I stood and caught eyes with Raiden, who stood by the edge of the showers. I didn't think he'd been one of the ones holding my brother under the burning spray, but I hadn't been focused on them, I'd been focused on Robbie. Anger burned on my face. "Coward," I spat.

Raiden looked like he might speak before he shook his head. He looked at Robbie before turning his back, casting one last glance over his shoulder. I swore I saw a tear streak down his cheek but he was gone before I could check. Coward.

I waited for Robbie to get to his feet on his own, turning my back to give him privacy as the shower turned on. It felt like hours before he stood next to me, towel around his waist, skin back to its normal hue.

"You okay?" I asked.

"The scouts . . ." Robbie inhaled, voice as shaky as his shoulders. "Did I blow it?"

I understood not to press. "Dad and Mom are doing damage control."

"Then it was worse than I thought."

"Everyone can have a bad game."

"You know that's not true."

And though I didn't want to, I said, "Yeah. I know."

Robbie bit his lip and walked past me to his stall. He pulled out his hockey bag and rooted through for his clothes.

"You know," I began, "You don't need to take it."

"Take what?"

"This sort of treatment. Maybe you should quit."

"Are you serious?" Robbie's head snapped up. "Hockey's the only thing I have left that doesn't make me want to . . ." He trailed off.

"All the draft stuff's making you miserable," I pressed. "Dad's making you miserable. The team—I mean. There are other choices out there."

"Easy for you to say. You don't love hockey," Robbie said. "I'd rather die than quit."

And in that moment, I understood why Robbie tried to kill himself.

My brother dressed quickly and silently. I rubbed my hands together as I waited. I knew he loved hockey, *breathed* hockey, but it was hard to imagine anyone putting up with this.

I was surprised to hear him say, "Wanna drive back with me?"

"Yeah. Yeah, sure," I said. We walked out to Robbie's car and got in it. I shot a quick text to Dad as a heads up, but he didn't reply.

As we drove, I wondered what to text Keisha about her party. There was no way we'd be able to go. Not after what Robbie endured. I already was trying to think of what to text her when Robbie asked, "So, what does semi-formal mean?"

"Huh?"

"For Keisha's thing. That's tonight, right?"

"You . . . still want to go?"

"Not really," he admitted. "But you want to."

"You just got the shit kicked out of you—"

"Thanks for reminding me," Robbie grumbled.

We drove in silence. "You really wouldn't mind? We don't need to stay the whole time, I just . . . want to see Keisha. Give her a present or something."

"I already said I'd go," he muttered. "Just leave it be."

And so, right or wrong, that's exactly what I did.

24

Even though the old cinema never played movies anymore, it was rented out for occasions, like corporate parties or birthdays. We walked through the double front doors. The lobby was filled with students. I saw Heather and Durrell dancing in a large circle with some of the other juniors and seniors. No one ever danced as couples unless it was a slow song. Just circles: big circles, little circles. Keisha was dancing in the big circle.

I stood watching, not sure if I should interrupt when she looked my way. She waved and wove through the group to give me a hug. Her hair was pulled up and curled, held back by a tiara, and she wore a short, blue dress, which complemented her dark skin. In heels, she was about my height, maybe even a tiny bit taller. "I'm *so* glad you guys could come!"

"Thanks for inviting us." I handed her a card with a gift certificate inside.

"Oh, Tristan, you didn't need to do that. I mean, you already wrote me that amazing story."

I shrugged and tried to play it off. "Well, I know. I mean, I just wanted to."

Keisha grinned, then set the envelope on a table that had some other presents on it. Robbie quietly put down the wrapped notebook he bought her, trying to push it behind some of the larger gifts. Keisha noticed, but beamed anyway.

"Come on," she said. "I want to introduce you to some of my friends from out of state." She linked her right arm with me and her left arm with Robbie before he'd have the chance to decline, and walked us across the lobby. Although there was a small group of students, one tall guy with a pink shirt and bright blue tie stood out. Robbie's eyes widened. He tried to pull back, expression on his face saying it all. *Mayday, mayday! Send help and abandon ship!*

"Tristan, Robbie, this is Kenny. Kenny, Robbie's the guy I told you about."

"Ooh, I see. Enchanted."

I had to bite my tongue. Kenny was the living stereotype of camp. The type of guy you'd look at and think, "Rainbows and unicorns and lisps, oh my!" Keisha pushed Robbie toward him. I watched my twin reluctantly shake Kenny's hand and turn his head toward the door as if he were plotting an escape route, but it was too late. Kenny started talking, hands wildly gesturing to accompany his words. Keisha tugged me away from them. I looked over my shoulder at Robbie, who gave me a death glare, while nodding and smiling fakely at Kenny as he tried to inch away.

"They could be really cute," Keisha said. I smiled but didn't have it in me to tell her that I doubted Robbie would be attracted to anyone *that* flamboyant. Then again, I didn't know what kind of guy Robbie liked. It's not like we talked about it or anything. I just assumed big men with muscle. Athletes, like the different Devils players in the posters on his walls. Like Adam Henrique, whom all the girls swooned over. Or maybe some sort of post-rock guy who also liked female piano rock musicians. Maybe sometime I'd ask him.

Across the empty cinema, Heather and Durrell were grinding in the circle of dancing students, occasionally making out as their bodies collided. PDA. Lovely.

Keisha asked, "Does it bug you that they're together?"

"No," I lied. I didn't want Keisha to think I was still into Heather, even if I still had some sort of attachment. But that attachment was slowly dissolving into hatred. "It bugs me that her personality did a one-eighty on me." I took a deep breath. "I'm really surprised you invited us after all the drama and stuff, you know?"

"I always wanted you to come. Robbie, too," she added quickly, not quite looking me in the eye. The bass from the DJ's speakers was loud enough for the ground to vibrate beneath my feet. Keisha swayed a little from side to side, not quite enough to be dancing in place. "I know it's kind of old and lame, but I love 90s music. Told the DJ to play as much as possible. Forget requests. Is that selfish of me?"

"It's your birthday," I said. "Besides, who doesn't like 90s music?"

Keisha glanced toward the dance circle, and sighed with a closed-lipped smile. "They look like they're having fun dancing."

My confidence might have been destroyed by Heather, but at least I knew how to take a hint. "Let's have fun then." I tugged Keisha toward the group. People parted to let us in, the birthday girl was the queen. A few pulses of music, and I realized we were right across from Heather and Durrell. For a moment, Heather and I locked eyes. Immediately, I turned to face Keisha and rested my hands on her hips to keep her close and try to keep Heather out of my sight. Behind Keisha's shoulder, Craig gave me a thumbs up before making out with some guy.

With each song, I got closer to Keisha. She really knew 90s music and sang along to everything, from Destiny's Child's "Jumpin' Jumpin" to Crush's "Jellyhead." I was surprised I knew almost as many of the lyrics as she did. When we weren't dancing or singing, we were laughing. I hadn't had that much fun with a girl since Heather. Hadn't really smiled since this mess with Robbie happened and our parents locked us away.

The music cut abruptly and the lights turned on. Was it the end of the night already? I was stock still, unsure whether I should pull away from Keisha or stay close to hide my tented pants.

Keisha took a step back and I hooked my thumbs in my pockets, pulling the fabric away from me, trying to think of boring things.

"You know," Keisha said. "I'm really glad you came, Tristan. Robbie, too."

"We should hang out more often. I mean, if you want."

"Yeah. I would."

From the corner of my eye, I saw Durrell watching me. He looked confused.

I took a deep breath, then pressed my lips to Keisha's cheek. "I'll see you in school or on Facebook or something, yeah?"

Keisha looked dazed for a moment by the kiss, then grinned and nodded. "How about both? And maybe outside of school, too?"

"It's a date," I said without thinking.

For a moment, I thought she might lean in and kiss me back, maybe with tongue, but she scooted away to wish her other guests goodbye.

I turned to the door, for a moment forgetting about my

brother until I saw him standing near it, making *HELP ME* gestures while Kenny continued to flourish with his hands. I cut over to him and patted Kenny on the back. "Sorry to cut in, but I've gotta head back and I'm his ride."

"Aww, that's too bad." Kenny grinned at Robbie. "I'll add you on Facebook."

"Right," Robbie said between grit teeth. He grabbed my arm and dragged me out the door. Beneath his breath, he hissed, "Remind me to find out his last name so I can block him before he gets the chance to add me."

"That bad?"

"He tried to talk me into watching *Glee* and *The New Normal*."

"The horror."

"I know, right? *Then* he had the nerve to tell me that hockey was a barbaric, primitive sport until I said I played it. Then he magically had a change of heart. And get this, when I asked him who he'd hypothetically root for, do you know who he said? Do you?"

Even though I knew the answer, I said, "Winnipeg Jets?"

"What? No. The jerk said he was totally a fan of the Rangers. You know how much I hate bandwagon New York fans? It's one thing if he grew up liking them, had parents who actually saw them win their last Cup, but no excuses!"

"Oh, come on."

"I could have overlooked the other issues, but that? That's crossing the damn line."

I couldn't help it. I burst out laughing. Robbie gave me a hard shove as we walked into the cold night's air. "It's not funny!"

"Oh, come on. You can't say that someone liking a rival hockey team is a deal breaker."

"Yes, I can!" he huffed, crossing his arms over his chest.

"Ever think about what would happen if you were drafted by the Rangers?"

Immediately, a look of horror crossed Robbie's face. "You don't think . . ."

"It could be payback." I knew I was pushing it, but I was in too good of a mood to resist. "Devils drafted Matteau's kid, Rangers draft—"

"Ugh. I hate you, Tristan. I really do."

Robbie shook his head crossly, but I kept smiling. How could I not? Keisha just made my night, no, my week even. Heather's expression was priceless. I was in a great mood, and Robbie could deal with a few miserable hours. It was the least he owed me.

Mom was in the kitchen on her cellphone when we came in. "How was the party?" she asked, not looking up.

"Amazing," I said without thinking about whether she really wanted an answer or not. Mom turned her body away. I guess she didn't. At least not from me. I'm not sure why I blurted out, "Keisha was really stoked that I was there. Danced with her the whole night."

Immediately, Mom whipped around. Her face lit up. I'd never seen an expression like this from her. Ever. "Who's Keisha? Birthday girl?"

"Yeah. She's this amazing girl in acting." When Mom twitched a little, I added, "Potential girlfriend. I mean, I hope. Nice, smart, beautiful—"

"Ugh," Robbie said. "You're going to make me barf."

Mom laughed. A rare, genuine laugh. She actually stood up and ruffled my hair. I wanted to twist my body and embrace her, but that would've been too much. We might have grown up starved for touch, but I'd take what small endearments I could get. The glow soon faded when Mom asked, "What about you, Robbie? Any potential girlfriends?"

Robbie stiffened. "No."

"Really?" Mom stepped away from me. "Doesn't seem fair that Tristan's getting all the attention, although Keisha sounds great."

"She *is* great," I said.

But Mom wouldn't stop. "I know you've been focused on the draft, but haven't you noticed someone?"

To Mom, Robbie being gay would be even more crushing than if I was. If she seemed that insulted by me acting, I couldn't imagine the rage if she knew about Robbie.

Robbie played with his fake lip piercing, like he was figuring out an excuse to take off. I felt a sudden pain in my chest, my lungs burning. Robbie's face stayed blank, but his silent screams overflowed and leaked into me.

Something was wrong.

I opened my mouth to speak but nothing came out. What could I say, especially in front of Mom? Before I could think of something, Robbie cut me off, surprising me as he said, "There's sort of someone . . ." His voice trailed off into a nothingness.

Before she'd have the chance to ask more, Robbie hustled up the stairs, shoving past Dad as he came down.

"What's with him?" Dad asked.

"Beats me," I lied, eyeing the stairs. If I took off right then after Robbie, my parents would know something was up. "I was telling Mom about Keisha. She's the girl whose party we went to." I felt in my pocket for my cell and pulled it out. I flipped through the photos before awkwardly holding my phone out. Mom reached for it first, but Dad closed his hand around the phone. He gazed at the pictures and flipped through, nodding his head.

"She's pretty," he said, totally disinterested before handing the phone to Mom.

Mom's finger hovered over the photos as she went through, the smile breaking with a hint of confusion.

"What's wrong?" I asked.

"Nothing," Mom murmured. "She's just . . . not what I expected. She seems nice. Good smile."

"What'd you expect?" I asked.

"Just . . . something else." Mom forced a smile then. "I'm glad you're dating a girl though."

A girl. Not *that* girl. Or *Keisha*. But *a* girl. Like any woman would be better than a man in her eyes.

I took my phone back and walked up the stairs to Robbie's room. He was already in pajamas sitting at his computer, weaving back and forth in the chair as he looked at the screen, headphones blasting. When he noticed me, he took his headphones off and hit pause. I was surprised that it wasn't some female, piano rock musician he was listening to but some clashing beat with a distinctly male voice.

"Who are you listening to?"

"There's this guy I've talked to a bit online," he mumbled.

"That Jimmy guy?"

"Yeah. He sent me a link to his band's demos. I think they're pretty good."

From what little I heard, they were pretty garbage.

"How was it with Mom and Dad and the girlfriend interrogation?" Robbie asked.

"Mom got really weird after I showed her pictures."

Robbie's lower lip puffed out. "You can't tell me you're surprised."

"Actually, I am."

"It's because she's black."

"Huh?"

Robbie shook his head. "Seriously, have you seen Mom with any friends who weren't waspy Stepford Wives?"

"No . . ." I murmured. "Durrell's been over before. She's never said anything about him."

"He plays hockey. He's great at it. And he's on D, so I'm not competing with him for a roster spot," he said. "She's probably caught in the dilemma deciding which is worse, having a gay son, or having her white son date a black woman."

"Jeez . . ." I sat at my computer.

Robbie twisted in his computer chair to face me. "Don't let it get to you. For what it's worth, I think she's attractive . . . you know . . . for a girl."

A smile cracked on my brother's face, enough to make me laugh. He got to his feet, stretched, and walked to his mattress.

"Go upload your stupid photos to Facebook and tag her, then get the lights. I'm tired as hell."

"About the party," I began. "Are you okay?"

"What do you mean?"

"I mean, is everything cool?"

Robbie got on his mattress and under the covers. "Yeah. It's cool."

"You sure?"

"Yeah. I'm sure."

My shoulders relaxed. I'd rather a false alarm than the alternative.

By the time I uploaded and tagged my photos and liked

every one that Keisha uploaded except the ones with Heather and Durrell, almost two hours had passed. Robbie was still, probably asleep. I got into bed.

If I were just a little bit braver, I would have kissed Keisha on the lips. Kissing Keisha properly would have to wait. She seemed to like the romantic, mushy stuff, and I kind of liked that, too. Maybe I'd take her out to some retro ice skating park with music from the 70s, 80s, and 90s. I didn't know if she skated, but if she didn't, it'd be a good excuse to have my arm around her for support and I could show off. I might have been crap next to my brother, but I'd be good to her.

Finally, things were going right.

25

I woke up to muffled screaming. For a few disoriented moments, I stayed on my mattress, not wanting to get up.
Monday mornings were always the worst. A cold breeze came
in from our window. I stood up, groggily stepped over the
mattress, and tugged at the wood. It wouldn't budge. "Hey
Robbie, help me get this thing shut?"

Silence.

I looked behind my shoulder; the mattress next to mine
was empty. From downstairs, there was more screaming:
louder, less muted.

I didn't stay in my room another second. My socks skidded on the floor when I sprinted out of my room and to the
stairs, still in my sweatshirt and pajama bottoms. The clock
chimed six times as I ran down the steps, echoing through
the long hallway.

But when I got downstairs, shouting, "Where's Robbie?"
he was right there. On the couch, arms folded across his chest.
At first glance, he looked normal, but a closer look showed
that his clothes were filthy, face scratched up and bruised.

"What's going on?" I demanded. "Robbie, what happened?!"

Mom and Dad whirled on me, stunned. Like they forgot I
lived in the house. They didn't need to answer. Their expres-
sions said everything I needed to know.

Robbie tried it *again*.

As if two suicide attempts weren't bad enough, now there was a third. If statistics on suicide were accurate, soon there would be a fourth, and a fifth, until finally he'd take it too far and there wouldn't be a next time.

My veins throbbed by my temple, skin burning hot from anger. We shared the same room, mattresses right next to each other on the goddamn floor. Last night, we had a great time. Why didn't he wake me up?

My body seized with hurt. This was just proof that Robbie and I would never be close. We weren't born close, so why should we get close now? The first time he tried to kill himself, I was numb. The second time he tried, I went to an audition and came back guilty as hell. My parents made me think I was the reason he couldn't cope. Robbie didn't try to commit suicide because of me. I had nothing to do with it.

Mom rubbed the bridge of her nose. She looked so weary and old. "The Dean is going to come here this afternoon so we can discuss a leave of absence."

"Car accident," Dad said wearily. "If she asks, it was a car accident."

"That'd be telling the truth," my twin muttered.

Unbelievable . . .

"Are you going to send Robbie to a psychiatric hospital?" I demanded.

"No." Mom looked at Dad, then said, "We're pulling both of you from school to focus on playoffs."

"Are you serious?" I gawked. "I don't even play hockey anymore!"

"You need to watch your brother."

"I'm eighteen. You can't make me."

"Actually, we can until you finish the school year, unless

you want to drop out, stay in a homeless shelter, and be cut off financially."

I'd had enough. If I was going to get grounded by proxy anyway, I would at least take the opportunity to speak my mind.

Mom asked, "Something you want to say, or are we clear?"

She hated questions. She hated when we answered questions. She hated when we asked them. I looked her dead in the eye.

"Yeah, actually." I clenched my fists. "What the hell is wrong with you? Why would you only take Robbie to the hospital once even though he's tried *three* times? Are appearances worth more than his life? He needs to be committed, or in therapy, or something!"

"Are you done?" Mom said in the way that meant discussion over.

"You and Dad, *especially* Dad, blamed *me* for Robbie trying to kill himself. What kind of demented parents blame their own child for something like that?"

"Tristan—"

"It wasn't my fault that Robbie tried to hang himself. I had *nothing* to do with it! *Nothing!* I went to one stupid audition. I didn't tell him to tie a noose around his neck!"

"That's unfair—"

But I couldn't stop. The brakes on my verbal locomotive wouldn't slow down. "If you don't acknowledge me as your son, then don't make me a scapegoat for your own shortcomings as parents!"

"Tristan, that's enough!" Dad yelled. "You're completely out of line taking this out on your mother."

"I'm out of line? Pot calling the kettle black? When the hell have you ever treated me like a son? When have you *ever* done anything for me?" I faced Mom. "Like you calling me a faggot because I like musicals and want to act. Or you judging Keisha because she's black."

Mom became pale. "I'm not racist or homophobic—"

"Maybe you're not if it's someone else's kid!" I snarled. "You know what I was doing after school while Robbie was at hockey practice? I was at rehearsals. Because that audition I did? Yeah. I booked a lead in the spring musical."

"Tristan—"

"Seriously, what's wrong with you two? Are you guys trying to win the worst parents of the year award? Because if you are, congratulations. I think you're in the lead."

Dad bunched his fists up like he was about to strike me. In his eyes, I didn't see anger. I saw guilt and the threat of tears. "One more outburst, and—"

I laughed. "And what? What else could you possibly take from me?" I started up the steps, but only made it halfway before I stopped and turned around. I leaned on the banister to glare at my twin. He gazed at me, eyes shiny with tears.

Looking him dead in the eye, I said, "I never thought I'd actually hate you."

I stormed up to the room, slammed the door, then waited. There was only silence. I pressed my ear to the door. Not a peep.

They weren't coming.

I fell on my mattress, buried my face in my pillow, and began to cry. They didn't care enough to follow me and see if I was okay, or even to punish me.

I screamed into my pillow, but I didn't feel better. Screamed again; still nothing. Although I didn't want to kill myself, at that moment I didn't want to live. What was the point? I was eighteen, and I was still a prisoner.

I pulled the covers over my head, closed my eyes, and

tried to force myself to sleep but I kept turning and shifting uncomfortably. I must have passed out at some point because the next time I opened my eyes, I felt someone watching. "Go away, Robbie."

"It's Dad."

I pulled the covers down from my face and rubbed dried snot off of my nostrils. "What do you want?"

Dad sighed, "Mind if I come in?" He didn't wait for me to answer before he stepped in and closed the door behind him. "I know this isn't fair for you. Your mom, too. Especially her. You really shook her up with the homophobic and racist thing."

"Good."

Dad hesitated. "Look. We're a small family. Your mom and I can only do so much. Robbie needs all the support he can get."

I stared at my dad incredulously. Did he really talk about Robbie's potential career as being a priority for *me?* That I needed to sacrifice even more? "Then send him to a therapist and leave me alone."

"He can't go."

"He can't play if he, you know, kills himself."

"He can't play if he doesn't get drafted. And he won't get drafted if . . ." Dad's voice trailed off. "No team's going to want a liability. If they think he's too depressed to function . . ." He looked me straight in the eye. "He's only got one shot to make it, Tristan. We all need to make sacrifices and this . . . it's just until the draft. Then he can get a therapist. If you're becoming an actor, you've got the rest of your life."

"Actually, I don't," I snapped. "Dancers only have so many years. If my voice isn't strong enough—" I couldn't finish. I hugged my pillow to my chest.

"Is there anything we can do to make it up to you?"

"Yeah. You can put me up for adoption," I muttered.

"Do you want to go get some lunch? I could take you and Robbie to get Chinese. Buy you guys some DVDs at the mall."

"Buy *us* some DVDs, yeah. That's making it up to *me*." I set my pillow down. "I want to do the musical."

"You need to watch Robbie."

"So you want me to chauffeur him to and from practice and won't let me go to my rehearsals, which, by the way, are at the same time."

"He's been a mess without you on the ice."

"He's not a mess because of me. He's a mess because the guys are beating the shit out of him for being gay."

As soon as the words left my mouth, I knew I fucked up. Big time. Dad stared at me. I couldn't read his expression. He took a few strides across the room to the closed door, opened it, and peered out. He shut it softly and sat on the mattress next to me.

I pressed my head in my hands. Outing someone was about the worst thing a person could do. It was Robbie's life to share, not mine.

"Robbie's gay?" Dad asked after several minutes. "Did he tell you?"

"He told everyone. He was trying to protect me from some of the football players." I bit my lip. ". . . please don't tell him I told you that. Or tell Mom."

"Damn." Dad swore. "Okay. Okay. So he said that to protect you. I can work with that. I'll contact the scouts and say it was in solidarity with you—"

I faced my Dad, jaw dropped. "You're going to say it's a lie?"

"He's got one shot," Dad said. "Once he makes it big, he can do what he wants. We'll just say you're gay. With you acting and quitting hockey, scouts would believe that. Robbie'll be the hero that way. Hell, his stock would probably go through the roof."

I got to my feet. "Get out."

Dad gazed at me, stunned. "But—"

"Get out," I reiterated with a growl.

He got to his feet. Then said, "I'll reimburse you for doing this—"

"I said, get out."

"Dance clothes? Equipment? Shoes? Lessons once the season's over?"

"Get out!" I yelled, pulling open the door. If there was one thing I knew, it was that I wouldn't ever give Dad the satisfaction of buying me over. "Get OUT!"

"Equipment, clothes, shoes, lessons once the season's over, and in the interim, I'll buy you Broadway tickets."

. . . except possibly that.

My lips tugged down. This had nothing to do with giving my parents satisfaction—but they owed me. Dance shoes were expensive. Dance clothes were expensive. Dance belts were expensive. Lessons were expensive. And Broadway shows were expensive.

"I still want to go to rehearsal," I said.

"Not happening, Tristan."

My lips pressed in a thin line. No, missing my chance was what's *not happening*. I could possibly sneak over to rehearsal while Robbie was in practice. Robbie owed me that much. I'd *make* him owe me.

"I'll write a list of what I need."

"Done."

"And I want one show a week."

"That's way too much."

"Let me go into the city by myself then."

"You need to stay with Robbie."

"So you're saying Robbie's coming with me to see musicals?"

Dad's forced smile disappeared. "Every month for the rest of the season."

"You want me to pretend I'm gay instead of my brother so he can get drafted *knowing* that Mom will treat me like hell?"

"She won't. If anything, she'll treat you better for what you're doing."

"How would—oh my god, Dad. You can't tell her."

"It's going to come out sooner or later. Better from me than the press."

I slumped low. No. It wouldn't be better from Dad than the press. It wouldn't be better unless it came from Robbie's lips.

"It'll be fine," Dad said. "And you'll get the benefit of a show every month."

"Every week," I mumbled. "To compensate for Robbie never speaking to me again."

Dad shifted his weight and sighed. "Every week unless there's a big game." He pulled out his iPhone and handed it to me. "Write a list of the dance supplies you need."

Reluctantly, I wrote out a list, everything from dance belts to tap shoes, to leg warmers. By the time I was done with essentials, there must have been over a thousand dollars worth of stuff on it. Good tap shoes usually ran at least three hundred dollars alone. I then wrote down as many extras as possible, from character shoes to unitards to stage makeup. Anything I could think of. I handed it to Dad. He didn't even flinch. "I'll order it right now. Glad we could get this all resolved."

But it wasn't all resolved. I'd just sold myself out.

"Why don't you see if there's something Wednesday night you want to see? We'll go right after practice. You, me, and Robbie."

The idea of spending time with Robbie right now wasn't appealing. At all. Or Dad. Especially both of them. But I wanted to see a show, and I was going to hold Dad to this. "I get to choose it without complaint, right?"

"Completely up to you."

Dad left, and I booted up my computer to look up shows. My heart sank when I saw a Facebook message pop up from Keisha: *Had a great time with you! I can't wait to see you at school!!! =)*

Reluctantly, I typed up my reply: *Hey Keisha, I had a great time, too. Thanks for inviting me. I hope we hang out again soon.* I rubbed my eyes. *Bad news, though. Mom and Dad are making us take a leave of absence.* I stopped typing, took a breath, and continued. *Robbie had another attempt. Not sure what all happened, but he totaled his car. We're only able to leave the house to go to practice.*

I hesitated, not quite sure what else to write. I didn't want to seem like I was whining, or blowing her off. And I didn't want to seem like I was gloating about being a superhero for watching my suicidal twin. *I'm going to sneak out at practice so I can go to rehearsal. See you there, I hope?* And, after a little thought, I added, *::Kisses Cheek::*

The door opened. Robbie came in, hair flat against his scalp from a shower. I didn't hear the shower on this floor. "They boarded up our bathroom," Robbie answered my unasked question. "Have to use the one downstairs."

"Why?"

"Because there's no Jacuzzi and therefore I won't drown myself, apparently."

"Don't you need to use a Jacuzzi for your muscles?"

"Apparently the one at the school's good enough. That is if I can get there alone." He shifted, trying to seem upbeat, though his voice betrayed him. "Dad said we're going to see

165

something on Broadway. Am I, uh . . . am I supposed to wear anything specific? Like a suit or anything?"

"Look dress code up yourself."

"I thought I'd just ask you."

"Well, don't ask."

"You don't need to bite my head off. You should be happy I'm seeing some lame ass musical with you."

"Happy? *Seriously?* After what you did?"

"You weren't there, Tristan. You have *no* idea."

"Actually I was *right here.* You could have woken me up."

"Get over it."

"No, fuck you."

Robbie sat down at his computer and started to type. I'm not sure why that got to me so much, but it did. Robbie wasn't acting any differently. Maybe Dad hadn't talked to Mom yet, or told Robbie that he knew. Or Dad said something, Mom went in denial, and nothing changed.

I went through the different Broadway shows and thought about the ones I'd enjoy that Robbie and Dad would be sure to hate. Especially Robbie. He was getting off easy, and he had no right to tell me the musical I liked was shit. If he made me miserable, he deserved to be equally unhappy. It came to me immediately. Not even a question. My face lit up, and I pulled my headphones off.

"Hey Robbie?" I said sweetly. "Ever hear of *Jesus Christ Superstar?*"

26

I couldn't believe it. He liked it. Robbie freaking liked *Jesus Christ Superstar*. Not just liked, but *loved*. And it wasn't just him either, but my Dad, too.

What. The. Hell?

Seriously, the Arizona Coyotes had a better chance of winning the Stanley Cup this year than Robbie or Dad—let alone both—liking *Jesus Christ Superstar*. Was there some alien abduction that I didn't know about? Were they the results of a recent brain transplant?

I wanted to be mad at them for liking it and having a good time, but I enjoyed the show too much and was on a high from its excitement and energy. I knew it'd be epic. I loved the soundtrack, and both the 1973 and 2000 films. But the films didn't have that sort of live energy. We even had an understudy on for Judas, and he stole the show.

Robbie couldn't even speak during intermission, just shook his head in astonished disbelief. Dad roared with laughter the moment King Herod's song came on and his buffoon followers danced wildly around a piano. All of us flinched as Jesus was flogged, watched the marquis turn red with electric blood as the bullwhip cracked through the air.

The car ride home was actually fun. Dad let us stop at Starbucks where we got *venti* skim chais, and then stopped at a sidewalk food vendor for giant pretzels and hot dogs. "What was your favorite part?" Robbie asked, mouth full of pretzel.

"Definitely 'Gethsemene.' Best song in the show," I said. "Yours?"

"Everything Mary sang." Not surprising. He always loved the female vocalists. "Oh, and the one Judas did at the beginning with the sick guitar riff."

"'Heaven on Their Minds.' That's a great one, too." It was kind of nice being the expert instead of the afterthought.

When we were near the house, Dad said, "I can't wait until the next show. Pick another great one, okay?"

Yeah. Okay. Fine. Next week, I'd make them sit through *Aladdin.*

The car rolled into our garage, and we parked and got out. I thought I heard Robbie say, "That was the best night of my life," but I probably imagined it. Like the last three nights didn't happen.

We said goodnight to Dad—Mom was already asleep— then went upstairs to get ready for bed. Although Robbie went straight to get his pajamas, I stopped in the doorframe. Something felt a little off. I looked around the room. The table had disappeared. I'm not sure how my parents thought Robbie could kill himself with that, but nonetheless it was gone. Our computers and printer sat on the ground. We pushed the mattresses farther apart, but that only made the room feel smaller. Pushed together against the side of the room closest to the window, we now had a small path.

I crossed the room and had trouble making the window budge. I gripped the frame and tried to pull up, but it wouldn't budge. "Hey, Robbie, help me out?"

Robbie walked to the window and gripped it, but even with his yanking, it didn't move. "The hell?"

I looked down at the windowsill, wondering how we could get the window open when I noticed a thin layer of something white against the painted frame. A sort of putty, or glue to keep the windows shut. "Oh, no . . ."

"What?" Robbie asked, then looked down at the sealant and looked sick. He touched his fingers against the wood. "Is this to keep me from jumping out?"

"No, it's so we suffocate," I said sarcastically. I walked away from the window and let myself drop on the mattress. "Great. Just great. Maybe we should get ourselves in trouble and get in juvie. We could at least get outside an hour a day that way."

"I'm sorry I tried to kill myself again," Robbie blurted out. His words caught me off-guard. He hurried to continue, "I just . . . couldn't cope."

"With what?"

"You'll get mad if I tell you."

"I'm already mad at you."

"I don't mean at me," Robbie muttered beneath his breath.

I waited, confused. If not himself, who? The hair on the back of my neck rose, but I wasn't entirely sure why. "Mom and Dad?"

"The party."

"Huh?" I sat upright. "What do you mean?"

Robbie shrugged and hugged his sides. "I don't know. Some stupid stuff happened at Keisha's birthday party. And I guess so soon after the loss . . ."

"I thought you spent the whole time with that Kenny guy."

Robbie snorted, "Hell no. I was trying to give him the slip. Thought I actually got away until I went in the bathroom to take a piss and he was there. Freaking stalker."

"So, what happened?"

Robbie rubbed his shoulder. "I ran into Heather without

Durrell." Robbie looked away from me. "Heather said something that kind of . . . hit home, I guess. I don't know. It was stupid. Never mind. Forget about it."

"Drop the cryptic crap. You're bad at it. What'd she say?"

"Tristan—"

"Just spit it out."

"She said if I actually did the job right, the team wouldn't have to suffer anymore."

Time stopped. That moment after an explosion where everything was silent. My throat clenched. "You're lying." *It's impossible . . .* "She would never say anything like that." *She wouldn't dare. That wasn't Heather. That wasn't my once best friend.*

"When have I ever lied to you?" Robbie asked desperately, gripping my shoulder. I tried to yank away from him, but he was stronger. He now clung to my arm, pleadingly, needing. "Name *one* time I've lied to you."

There must have been something. Must have been some time Robbie lied to me and I caught him at his bluff. But I couldn't think of an instance. Even when Robbie used to gang up on me, taunting me, harassing me, he was honest. Bluntly so.

Robbie would never lie, not about something like that. If anything, Robbie would be silent. Like the way he was after we went to Heather's and she talked about the man who hanged himself in the guest room while we watched *The Virgin Suicides.* Like the way he was about being gay when he kept trying to tell me that he didn't think he could hide *it.* That he couldn't lie to his teammates about his sexual orientation if they asked. That he liked guys. Men.

Robbie's shoulders dropped. "I couldn't do it, Tristan. I tried, but I couldn't."

"Why?" I whispered, thinking of Heather. She used to

talk about how depressed bullying made her feel. How school shootings and suicides could be prevented if people just smiled a little bit more and stayed a little less vicious. Didn't she? It was hard to remember the way we used to be friends, the personality that suddenly became bitch extraordinaire.

"Because I got scared shitless, all right?" Robbie snapped. "I'm sorry, okay? You know how fucking terrifying it is driving into oncoming traffic, realizing you could hurt someone else, and not knowing when you spun the wheel to the side of the road whether you'd make it without killing an innocent bystander?"

"Huh?" I blinked up from my reverie, realizing then how my words must have sounded. Robbie misunderstood my why, thinking I was asking about why he didn't kill himself properly. "I—no, I meant why to Heather. She's . . . different, you know?"

"Oh . . ." Robbie's face contorted like a gargoyle's as he tried to refrain from crying. I wanted to say something else, to change the subject instead of hear what Robbie was about to say, but there was no stopping now. Not when Robbie was fighting to even get his words out. If I stopped him now, Robbie would never talk again.

"Instead of things getting normal, everything got revoked. Your life sucks even more than it did because I chickened the hell out. And people don't get it. Think about what would happen to me." Robbie trembled faintly. "Legally, I could play, I know that. I've seen players get reprimanded with fines and tiny suspensions, but for how long? If they learn not to say the word "faggot" or "queer," they'll just figure out something else to say. And the fans . . ." Robbie rubbed his hands over his face. "Remember when Zach Parise left for the Wild, and Minnesota passed gay marriage bills, all the fans went off about how much of a homo he must have been? Because that's the worst thing they can think to say—not traitor, not deserter, but *gay*. Millions of people all ripping on this guy just because he wanted to go home . . . That's the scariest part. More than the players. The fans."

I swallowed hard. My mouth was too dry to speak. Everyone always talked about the homophobia in professional sports. If harassment on Facebook from classmates was bad, how much worse would it be if he got famous?

"Maybe you're right. Maybe I should quit hockey."

I struggled to breathe. It was too much to process at once. *Robbie* was too much to process at once. Him? Quit? Quitting his lifeline? Because of me?

My twin looked at me hopefully, wishfully, wanting me to say something. To deny his words, grant him forgiveness. He was silently begging for mercy that I couldn't give. I didn't know how. I didn't deserve to be the one to grant him that.

"I . . . need to use the bathroom," I squeaked.

My brother's composure dissolved. He lay back on the mattress and pulled the covers up over his head, curling on his side so his back faced me.

Mechanically, I got up from my mattress and stepped over his. I went down the steps into the spare bathroom and changed into my pajamas. I stared at the mirror, wondering what I could say, but there was nothing. Even after splashing water over my face, my thoughts wouldn't clear. I tried to digest what Robbie said, but as each sentence revolved through my head, I felt even worse. If I hadn't let Robbie speak, I would have told him to look up an organization, to get help. I would have told him, "It gets better," because that was what everyone was supposed to say. Because it was supposed to get better. Saying that was like saying, "Hang in there," or "Try harder."

But my brother had been hanging in there. He'd done his

research, tried to find a way that he could fit in, and there was a problem. He studied the fans, his possible future in the NHL. He'd seen up close the cutthroat nature of teenagers desperate to make the league, others be damned.

When I returned to my room, I hit the lights and went straight to bed. Usually, I checked my email and Facebook first, but this time I wanted to crawl under the sheets to hide. Robbie's shaky breaths rattled like the wind outside our windows. I looked at his feet, then grabbed my pillow and turned around on my mattress. Setting the pillow on the same side of the mattress as Robbie had on his, I turned on my side. "Hey, Robbie?"

Dark shadows mostly hid Robbie's face, but I was certain he was crying. It made me feel worse. I caused that. He wanted to confide in me, but I couldn't play therapist.

I complained about not being close with my brother, with being frustrated with him, and yet, when he needed me, I pushed him away. Maybe some hidden part of me didn't want to get to know Robbie better. Maybe that part of me wanted us to stay strangers. Or maybe I was just terrified about what would happen if we were friends.

"Just wanted to tell you that was a great show," Robbie eventually whispered. He was a much better person than me.

"Yeah. It was."

I hesitated a moment, then leaned forward and wrapped an arm around Robbie in a half-hug. Almost as soon as I did, I pulled away and turned on my side, my back to him. I could have sworn he said *thank you* in my head, but the room was silent. It was only when I was certain he was asleep that I decided I'd say I didn't hate him. But the only whisper that came off my lips was, "Goodnight."

27

After I dropped Robbie off at practice, I went to the front office to pick up our coursework and outlines from our teachers. Amazing what a private school was willing to do in exchange for bragging rights about a huge championship. The secretary, Mrs. Samson, looked at me with absolute pity the second I stepped into the office. I didn't even need to say my name or what I was there for.

"I'll have your work in just a second, Tristan. You're Tristan, not Robbie, right?"

"Yeah. He's the one with the bleach."

"I thought so," Mrs. Samsom said as she opened a filing cabinet and pulled out two stacks. They were smaller than I thought as I skimmed through.

"Is this really it?" I asked.

"That should be. It's a good thing you both have terrific grades—most of the faculty offered to waive some of your assignments."

My lips pursed together. Only one of us had terrific grades. Robbie wasn't as stupid as he thought he was, but he didn't really apply himself. NHL or nothing. Dad didn't exactly discourage him, though Mom mentioned that Boston College had a great hockey program.

"By the way," Mrs. Samson said before I left, "I hope everything works out."

I left the office wondering what lie my parents told the school. All of this for Robbie's career.

Outside, the air was frigid as I got in my car and returned to the arena. Halfway there, I turned around and went back to the main building. The car was barely stopped before I took off, panting hard as I burst into the auditorium. Everyone stopped blocking a scene—Heather perched high in the air in a lift. Ms. Price scrambled offstage and immediately made a beeline to me. "Tristan, I got a notice from the Dean that you were taking a leave of absence."

I lowered my head like it was the right thing to do. "My parents are making me keep an eye on Robbie because . . ." My voice trailed off. I could end it here. Say something, push for my twin to get the therapy he so desperately needed. But what if that meant he wouldn't get drafted? After all this—the hell, the torture—he deserved to be that high pick more than ever.

Ms. Price gazed at me, biting her lip as she waited for me to continue. I pictured returning to the house. Dad locking me in the room for ruining Robbie's life.

I shuddered. No. I couldn't say it. I couldn't.

"I know my parents kind of screwed up everything and you probably hate me, but I was hoping that maybe you'd let me be in the ensemble. Or even a stage hand or something."

Ms. Price was silent for a long time. I didn't know if that was a good or a bad thing. "Are you supposed to even be at rehearsal?"

"No," I said truthfully. "I dropped Robbie off at practice. I was supposed to watch him to make sure he—" I stopped myself. "I was just supposed to watch him."

Ms. Price hesitated. "How old are you?"

"Eighteen."

"So, you can legally make decisions for yourself."

"Yes."

"Yet your parents are controlling this school situation?"

"Just until we graduate . . ." *I hope.*

Ms. Price rubbed her hand over her mouth. "This is extremely unorthodox, but I'm an unorthodox teacher." She wrapped her arms around me in a tight hug. "I didn't give away your part."

I stiffened. "You're joking."

"I was going to talk to your parents and beg them to let you stay," Ms. Price confessed. "You have no clue how much we need you in this show. I know it's a steep learning curve with the tapping but do you know how incredible it is that you actually know how to skate? You can skate, sing, dance—adding tapping to your portfolio can only help. And once things settle down, I'll help you get some lessons in tumbling. Then you'll be extra set."

Even though I wanted to jump and scream and dance with joy, I hung my head. "I'm not sure what my limitations are going to be through the end of the season." *Or the draft,* I suddenly thought, tensing up. Would it be like this until Robbie committed to a team in juniors? Or if he made a surprise decision to do college hockey instead?

"Come to as many rehearsals as you can. I'll film the rest and send you Youtube videos. The show's in late May, so it'll be tough, but you can pull it off if you work hard. Are you willing to work hard for me?"

I didn't even pause. "Yes. Absolutely."

"Then there's no issue, especially when you really only

have two songs." Ms. Price gestured me to the stage. "Get out your scripts, everyone."

On stage, I saw Keisha sitting on the floor. Immediately, I crossed and sat next to her. Ms. Price began to go through blocking before I could really say hi. Keisha scooted closer to me until we were almost touching.

We went through lines, scribbling notes in pencil and sharing hi-lighters with a formal table read. At the end of rehearsal, I glanced at my watch, then at Keisha, gesturing with my chin for her to come with me. Without looking at each other, we gathered our bags and slipped into the hall, barely getting to the first set of lockers before I turned to her and she stepped into me. Arms around each other, foreheads touching, breathing each other in. She was so close, I could kiss her.

My pocket vibrated. Reluctantly, I stepped back and felt in my pocket for my iPhone. It was Robbie:

I'm done.

Done.

What kind of done? Done with practice done? Or done *done?*

"I gotta go. I'm sorry," I told Keisha.

"Is everything okay?"

"I don't know."

"Let me know if I can do anything, okay?"

"I will. I promise." I walked toward the door before turning back to her. With a few fast steps, she was in front of me. My lips touched her cheek. Before she could say another word, I was out the door, tugging my coat around me. I crossed the parking lot to the rink and slipped inside, rubbing my hands together for warmth as I wove to the locker room.

"Why are you avoiding me?"

My brother's voice stopped me dead in my tracks. I probably

should have retreated, given him a moment of privacy. But what if this was another red flag for, "I'm going to try it again?"

Another voice met his, "Why didn't you tell me?"

Raiden.

"I didn't know how you'd take it."

"I deserved to know. I wouldn't have . . . just I deserved to know."

"I didn't want you to hate me."

"Might be late for that."

"So what? You're going to hate me just because I'm gay?" Robbie's voice rose in volume and pitch. "You're going to ignore me on the ice, in the locker room, everywhere, because I like dick?"

"I told you, I don't care what you like."

"Then why are you treating me like shit?"

There was a silence. Then Raiden's voice was laced with some sort of strain.

"Do you seriously not remember?"

Remember what?

There was a silence, then some sort of sound, like Robbie gasping. "Fuck. Raid, I . . ."

I inched down the hall, trying to be as silent as possible.

"You're such an asshole sometimes, Robbie."

Then Raiden burst around the corner, hockey bag slung over his shoulders, almost knocking me over. Shortly after came Robbie, barreling down the hall. "Wait! Raid! Raid, wait up! I'm sorry! Wait!" He saw me too late, body propelled by inertia he couldn't slow. I hit the floor hard and wheezed, Robbie on top of me, crushing me.

Robbie stared at me, wide eyed and scared, before he got to his feet and extended his hand to me. I took it and he pulled me to my feet.

"Sorry," he mumbled.

"What was that about?"

Robbie looked away from me. "Can we just go home and pretend you didn't see that?"

"Sure," I said. Because if there was one thing I could do and do well, it was pretend. If only pretending meant forgetting as well.

28

When we got home, Mom was standing in the kitchen next to Dad. One glance from Dad, and I knew what was coming. I wanted to tell Robbie to run, to get out of the kitchen, to take my car and get as far away as possible.

I outed Robbie to Dad. Dad outed Robbie to Mom. Mom wasn't going to take it well.

"Hey," Robbie said wearily as he got two Gatorades from the fridge. Mom crossed the room in the short time it took for him to turn around. I thought about Robbie's fight with Raiden. I prayed she would let it go. *Not today. Not today.*

"I expected better of you," she said.

"Huh?"

Mom was a bit greenish. "Gay? Really?"

Robbie's fingers tightened around the bottles of Gatorade. Then Mom did something I never expected her to.

"Deny it," Mom begged. "Tell me your father's wrong. Please tell me he's wrong. You're not gay. Say you're not. *Please.*"

Robbie didn't speak.

Mom looked on the verge of tears. Or screaming. It was beyond heartbreak. "It's Raiden, isn't it?"

"Leave him out of this," Robbie spluttered. There was a pit in my stomach.

"I knew it." Her fists bunched up. "I knew there was

something not quite right. He just . . . he confused you. That's all."

"Leave him out of this. He didn't do anything."

"He did. You were fine. You were normal. "

"I'm still normal."

"No. You're not. This isn't normal. *He's* not normal. He corrupted you—"

"I initiated it!" Robbie bellowed.

There was a silence in the room. I couldn't move.

"I didn't know you were that sick," Mom whispered through tears. Mascara painted her cheeks like watercolor. "You know, when your father told me, I thought Tristan was lying for attention. Now I see he was just trying to do the right thing."

Robbie's head snapped to me. He slammed the bottles of Gatorade on the table, eyes fiery like coal. I knew what was going to happen before it did. I knew that face from my nightmares years ago.

I turned on my heel, running full speed. Robbie was after me in a flash, catching up to me before I could get a quarter up the stairs. He gripped my shoulders hard and wrenched me back down. I hit the wall moments before the first punch came.

"You TRAITOR!" he screamed, fist slamming into my face again. "TRAITOR!"

"It was an accident! I didn't mean to—"

Robbie's fist connected with my ribs, the same spot where weeks ago Eric had kicked me. I felt something sharp in my chest, a searing pain, and gasped shallow and hard as I dropped to the floor and curled on my side.

Immediately, Robbie's face paled. He was yanked back by Dad. "Let it go," Dad said. "Tristan, stop overacting."

I shook my head, continuing to wheeze.

"Tristan, I said knock it off."

To my surprise, Mom pushed past Robbie and knelt by my side. She pulled up my shirt enough to see the area and touched it with her fingers. If I had the breath, I would have howled.

She moved my arm around her shoulder and helped me to my feet. "Stop being a baby. You'll be fine."

My ribs felt cracked in two. "But—"

"Knock it off." She led me to the couch. I sank down on the plush cushions.

Robbie looked like he was going to vomit. "Tristan, I'm so, so sorry. I didn't—"

"Go to your goddamn room," she said, sitting on the edge of the couch near me. Robbie hesitated near the stairs. "*Go,*" she said harshly before he walked up as slowly as he could. Dad disappeared into the kitchen.

"It was my fault," I said, once Mom and I were alone. "I outed him."

"You did your obligation. You knew something was wrong, and your father overlooked you. Your father brainwashed me into overlooking you."

My head spun. How had it turned into something like this? "It's not wrong."

"It is. But not for the reasons you think. You know the pictures on the mantel of your Uncle Anthony?"

I was confused. "The one we never met who died of cancer?"

Mom gazed ahead. A tear slid down her nose.

"It wasn't cancer."

"But you told us—" My voice trailed off as things started to connect.

Mom's hatred wasn't about homosexuality at all.

It was about AIDS.

"Just because Robbie's gay doesn't mean that he's going

to get anything," I said. "I mean, you know that. Protection, safety. It's not like it's a gay thing. I mean, a lot of straight couples have HIV too—"

"I have to reduce the risk."

"You can't make him not gay."

"Do you know what it's like to watch your brother wither up and die?" Mom asked.

Almost, I didn't say.

"Losing Anthony was one of the hardest things I've ever experienced. I just . . . I don't want you to lose a brother, either."

"If he doesn't get help, I *will* lose my brother."

Mom got up and patted me on the knee. She looked like she was about to say something else when we heard the thuds of Robbie coming down the steps. A moment later, he appeared in the living room. "I'm not leaving until I can properly apologize," he said, eyes red.

I thought Mom might yell at him to go back upstairs. But she didn't. Instead, she walked out of the room, not even looking at him.

"I'm sorry I punched you," Robbie said.

"I deserved it."

"You didn't deserve to get the crap kicked out of you—"

"I told you, I deserved it. It was an accident, but I deserved it. When Dad told me about pulling us out of school, I just lost it. I didn't even know what I was saying. It just came out."

We gazed at each other. Softly, Robbie said, "It's fine." Then, "It'll *be* fine, unless she tries straightening me out."

"She told me why."

"Why what?"

"The whole homophobic thing. It's not really about being gay."

Robbie shot me an incredulous look. ". . . riiiiiiight."

"No, I mean . . ." I rubbed the back of my neck. "Uncle Anthony died of AIDS."

"Uh, no, stupid. He died of can—" The gears churned in Robbie's head. "Oh, son of a bitch."

"Yup."

"Is that why she . . . ?"

"Maybe she wanted something to blame for her brother getting sick and dying. It's probably why she freaked about me getting into acting, too. She doesn't want to go through it again."

"Damn . . ." Bizarrely, Robbie looked relieved. He almost smiled. "But that's good. Seriously good. Better to know she's afraid of me dying from AIDS than thinking I was going to hell when I die."

"We're all afraid of you dying," I said quietly. Robbie stiffened.

"Well," he said, changing subject, "it's for the better. All of this, really. It's easier to deal with scouts if everyone knows."

I swallowed hard, like gravel was caught on my tonsils. ". . . they're not going to know."

"What do you mean?"

"Dad wants me to take the fall."

"I don't understand."

"You found out I was gay and covered for me to be in solidarity. You didn't have the heart to tell the team you weren't because you didn't want me to get bullied."

"Are you serious? Why didn't you tell me?"

"Because I sold out. You know all those things Dad got me? That was compensation. I wouldn't have but I didn't want you to go lower in the draft because of me."

Robbie took a few moments to recollect himself. "I don't know if I want to lie," he finally said.

"But your career . . . I mean, Mom and Dad—"

"They can't fix this one," he said, walking to the stairs. He looked at me from the railing halfway up. "But hey, at least they have one straight son."

My twin tried to smile, but it was plastic and fake. It burned.

LATER THAT afternoon, I finally got off the couch. I walked upstairs to my bedroom, wincing with each step. My parents told me to stop overacting, but it seriously hurt to breathe. There was no point in staying downstairs, away from my brother. When I opened the door to his room, Robbie sat on his mattress, his back to me, shoulder moving strangely in some sort of jerking motion.

"Robbie?" His head snapped back, and Robbie yanked the sleeves on his hoodie down.

I sat next to him. "When Mom brought it up, you said something about Raiden."

"She was blaming him." Robbie fidgeted with his sleeves.

"You were fighting in the locker room. He said he didn't hate you because you were gay."

Robbie was silent.

I took a deep breath. "Did you . . . have something?"

Robbie continued to tug at his sleeves. Dampened his lips, but couldn't speak. I hesitated before reaching out to Robbie. "Let me see it."

"No." Robbie tried to keep his arms away from me.

"Let me see it," I insisted, seizing his wrist. Robbie winced. With a deep breath, I tugged his sleeve back. Robbie had a pair of Mom's manicure scissors in his palm. The tiny metal blades were red. My throat was dry. I reached for Robbie's other hand.

"Don't," Robbie pleaded, but I didn't listen and tugged up the opposite sleeve. Shallow lines sliced his arm. Not deep enough for serious damage, just some sting. Little lines of red, tiny beads clinging to them like dew drops on a spider's web.

"Robbie . . ."

I plucked the scissors from his palm and watched his body round over. He bit his lip, the piercing disappearing in his mouth for a brief moment, the way a fish might toy with a hook. A bit of jerkbait. Robbie ducked his head. His blond hair fell in his face, half-hiding his dark eyes. My patience reeled him in.

"It was just once," he confided, so soft I could barely hear him. "At Heather's when we had that team party. We were drinking, I mean, he was drinking. I didn't touch a drop. We went up to that guest room so he could smoke weed but there was this porn DVD sitting on the TV. So we put it on. And Raiden's all drunk, and he's getting hard and stuff and I'm getting hard because he is. I was joking and all saying we should jerk off since we were into it. Except I wasn't. But he's all, 'sure, no homo.' He was looking at the porn, I was looking at him. And I just—"

"Did you two—"

Robbie hung his head. "No. Maybe if he were sober, I would have asked . . ." He inhaled sharply. "I took advantage of a situation."

"You didn't touch him," I said. "If you did and he was drunk, that's one thing. But you just—"

"That doesn't mean I didn't take advantage of him."

I knew I should say something to console him. But the only thing that came out of my mouth was, "I'm sorry."

"Yeah. Me, too."

With Robbie's silence, I rose to my feet. "Hold on." I left the room then seized rubbing alcohol and a box of Band Aids from the medicine cabinet. Robbie's eyes squeezed shut, like he was trying to hold back tears, when I closed the door, sat next to him, and started to clean his wounds. "Sorry about the sting."

"It doesn't hurt," Robbie said. I looked in his eyes for a moment and believed him. There were no barriers between us. There was no reason to lie.

29

I was on the way to my car after rehearsal when I heard footsteps behind me. "Hey," Keisha called. "Wait up!"

"Hey. What's going on?"

"You're going to pick up Robbie, right?"

"Yeah. Why?"

"Can I come? I've got something for him."

She walked with me to the car, so close I should have reached out and grabbed her hand. Instead, I opened her car door then got in. By instinct, I reached to turn off the music. She put her dark hand over my pale one. "What are you listening to?"

"*Carrie: The Musical.* I can turn it off."

"Keep it on. I like campy shows."

I nodded and slowly drove through the parking lot toward the arena, maybe slower than necessary just to spend more time with Keisha. When I parked, Robbie was waiting for me outside and walked over. He looked a bit confused when Keisha got out of the passenger side.

"I just wanted to say I'm sorry about what happened with the party," she said, pulling off her backpack. She reached in and pulled out a loosely wrapped bundle. "My uncle works at the Prudential Center, so it wasn't too much, I swear."

I peered over her shoulder as Robbie opened the paper.

The red and black fabric was clearly a jersey. The back was signed with the inscription, "To Robbie, Best of Luck This Season! Adam Henrique, 14."

Robbie stood perfectly still before he lifted his head and squealed, "OH MY GOD!" Faster than I'd ever seen him move, he wrapped his arms around Keisha tightly. Even before the depressed, quiet persona kicked in, Robbie was never the type to bounce around in glee. "YOU ARE FREAKING AWESOME! I love you. Forget Tristan. You're my new best friend."

Keisha laughed as she patted Robbie's back. "Well, I'm glad you like it."

"I love it enough that I'd actually consider making out with you if Tristan didn't have such a boner for you. Well, and if I, you know, liked girls."

Keisha burst out laughing and pretended to slap Robbie. Her cheeks tinted faintly with a blush. I was certain my cheeks were burning.

"Anyway, I won't keep you held up," she said.

"Do you want a ride back to the parking lot?" I asked desperately.

"You know, as much as I'd like to say yes, it's actually nice enough to walk. I love when it's just starting to snow." She stepped to me and gave me a hug. "I'll see you at rehearsal, right?"

"Yeah. Absolutely." I wrapped my arms around her, palms sweaty. The fruity scent of her hairspray was similar to what Heather used to use. Coconut. The pain of nostalgia hit my stomach. Why did I have to think of that right then? I felt soft pressure on my cheek. Keisha's lips. A little kiss.

My eyes squeezed shut. If I didn't take the opportunity, I might never get the balls to do it. Before Keisha could turn away, I leaned in quickly and pressed my lips to hers. Our noses collided. There was the clink of teeth. I felt her clear, plastic retainer. We pulled away from each other abruptly.

Our first kiss, and I absolutely butchered it.

"I'll, uh. I'll call you." I said meekly, looking at the ground with hot cheeks.

"I'd like that," Keisha replied. "A lot."

I shuffled toward the car. We got in, me watching Keisha walk away. Robbie taunted. "Giiiiiiirlfriend."

"Shut up."

"What? I think it's cute."

"As cute as Henrique is to you?"

I jabbed Robbie in the side, and he tugged his autographed jersey away from me. After a few moments, he replied, *"Touché."*

I smirked victoriously. It was nice to be in that good a mood, to joke around and not have to worry about what Robbie might do. At that moment, I could relish kissing Keisha for the first time, awkward as it was. The next time would be smoother. Maybe next time, it could be just me and Keisha, without Robbie.

30

I sat in our room trying to work, but the monotony of our tiny prison made it hard to focus. Every few minutes, I'd refresh Facebook and Gmail, reading everything that arrived. Penis enlarger pills. An inheritance from a Nigerian prince. Something from a petition website. This was my life now. I'd drive Robbie to each hockey practice before taking off across campus to get to the auditorium for rehearsal. Two hours of bliss that left my body aching and voice sore. Two hours rehearsing alongside Keisha.

The moment rehearsal was over, Keisha and I would take off down the hall, hand-in-hand, across the parking lot and into the backseat of my car. We'd kiss, hard. Me on my back, Keisha on top of me, me making an effort to not grind against her until she shifted her weight and it was there, right there, four layers of fabric separating us. Reckless dry humping in the backseat of my car. It wasn't long—one minute, two minutes, five—before my phone would buzz, a text from Robbie saying he was ready. I'd drive Keisha to her car, we'd kiss one last time, then I'd drive to the arena. Robbie would get in, and we'd go back.

"You know, if you want more time with Keisha, you could just ask," Robbie said one night as we drove back.

I'd wanted to ask him how he knew, but Robbie just gave

me the look. Another time, he reached into the glove compartment, grabbed an old napkin, and rubbed it over my mouth to get lipstick off like I was a child. "They'll kill you if they know you're not watching me," he'd explained.

Robbie, my brother. Robbie, my co-conspirator.

I wondered what he thought we were up to, if he knew it was only making out and some dry humping, my shaking hands afraid to stray from her back, her waist, once the back pockets of her skinny jeans, which made me come, sudden, fast, and left me red-cheeked and embarrassed and hoping she didn't notice. I was always scared of kissing her neck in case I left a hickey, or that I didn't know what to expect if I felt her up. I think she'd say yes, if I asked. Maybe the next time I would.

AS PLAYOFFS approached, the intensity increased, especially as our winning team hit a sudden losing streak. This was the second to last game. We needed to win both to get into the playoffs, and that'd be only by a point. It was absolutely critical.

The past few games had been painful. I watched as my brother tried to adjust to the lack of me. He wasn't as bad as the first game after I quit. He looked good, but not superstar great. Dad had not been quiet in reminding Robbie that the last game before playoffs would be filled with scouts and that he needed to get his act together soon.

Tonight, the crowd was lackluster, barely cheering through the first two periods as we went down 2-1. Near the beginning of the third, my brother skated up to take the faceoff. From afar, I could see his opponent yapping. The second the puck dropped, Robbie and the opposing center's gloves came off, sticks on the ground, helmets thrown off as they lunged toward each other.

It took both linesmen to pull Robbie off of the other guy

and send both to the penalty box. When Robbie returned to the bench, our team tapped their sticks.

Even from a distance, I knew they were stick tapping the other team.

What the hell had the center said to him?

With the next few shifts, Coach yelled at Robbie to get faster and lighter. He was trying hard, so hard, but the spark was gone. *He* was gone.

Then it happened.

With eleven seconds left, I heard Robbie's name. My brother didn't even turn his head as he took off down the ice, with Raiden alongside him. They made eye contact moments before Raiden passed Robbie the puck. A switch flipped on.

Seven seconds.

I leaned forward. My brother lit up, the deadness in him vanishing. He deked past their defenders with ease and shot the puck. Their goalie knocked it back with his blocker.

Four seconds.

The puck bounced on the ice and my brother drew his stick back. Instead of shooting, he dragged his toe to the side in his signature move. Propelled with momentum, the goalie went down as Robbie flipped the puck up top shelf.

One second.

The lights above the goal lit up.

End buzzer.

Overtime.

Victory.

Game over.

31

"The room's smaller."

I took off my headphones and looked at Robbie. He paced the perimeter, stepping over the mattress and our clothes strewn on the ground. He touched the wall. "I swear to God, the room's smaller."

"That's impossible, Robbie."

"No seriously, Tristan. The room's smaller."

I folded my arms over my chest with a heavy sigh. True, the room felt smaller, but so did the house. Just confinement. Claustrophobia. Even though our calendar said a week passed, I couldn't distinguish time. Isolation was changing me. I wasn't able to listen to most of the musicals I used to love. Their happy lyrics and dance numbers made me feel more miserable and alone. I longed to be part of a happy group, to be preparing for a musical, or a play, or something. The characters in my stories were poor substitutes for company. More specifically, they were poor substitutes for Keisha. Rehearsals and a few minutes of fun weren't enough.

I looked around the room, our tiny, hellish room, before it hit me. "I know how we can get out."

Robbie watched as I pulled out my abandoned hockey bag and skates. "What are you doing?" he asked.

"Grab yours, come on."

I took off down the steps, slowing down just enough to make sure that Robbie indeed was coming after me as I went to the front door.

"Where do you think you're going?" Dad asked, appearing around the hall corner like he'd been waiting.

I held up my skates by the laces. "Practice. Pond froze over."

Sure enough, Dad nodded and went back to the newspaper, muttering, "Good, every little bit helps." I pulled on my heavy coat, beanie, and gloves as I waited for Robbie to do the same, then led us out the door.

We trudged in our boots to Hollow's Pond, just a few blocks from our house. Dad used to take us skating here when we were kids. It was frozen over. We slipped our skates on and skated over the fresh ice. My legs felt a little stiff through the first few laps, but as I warmed up, it felt easier; the ice was different than our school arena after the Zamboni slid by, but I liked it, liked the way my blades cut into it. More important, there were no walls out here.

As I changed direction, my feet grew lighter, my hips shifting. By instinct, I slipped into my choreography and sang to "An Accident Waiting to Happen." I heard Robbie roar with laughter and stopped, ready to defend myself when I saw he wasn't laughing at me but something on his phone.

Never had Robbie's phone took precedence when he had his skates on and ice below him.

"What's so funny?" I called.

Robbie looked at me and shoved the phone back in his pocket. "Sorry. Jimmy just said something funny."

"Who?"

"Jimmy. You know the guy with the band?"

"Right . . ."

Robbie finally pushed out and did some fast laps and hard

stops, stretching his limbs. Fast. Attack. Sharp. He drifted off
into his zone, and I returned to the choreography, singing a
bit louder as I twisted on the ice. It was hard to pretend not
to skate well or be uncoordinated. It's one of the reasons why
the best dancers often played the clumsiest characters, like
Craig getting Aldolpho.

"Holy shit." Robbie skidded to a stop in front of me.

"What?"

"I didn't know you could sing. You're freaking amazing."

I scanned his face for deception, but he looked awestruck.
But that awe vanished as he patted his pocket for his cell again.

"Dude, come on," I said. "We're finally out of that damn
room and you want to spend it texting?"

"I'm chatting," he said. "On AIM. And it's not like it's
hockey practice. Just . . . us, you know?" Robbie hesitated before handing his iPhone over, granting me brief permission
to see into his life. Jimmy's avatar was small and grainy. He
had dyed blue hair and a goatee.

"Isn't he hot?" Robbie asked. "I mean, he's not an athlete
or anything, but that's okay."

"Uh, I'm not necessarily the best judge of that."

"Hypothetically," he insisted. "If I can hypothetically say
Keisha's attractive, don't you agree about Jimmy?"

"Uh . . ." I squinted at the grainy photo. Hypothetically,
I still didn't think the guy was attractive. At all.

Robbie frowned. "I mean, he's not a model or anything,
but I dig the hair."

"He looks older than twenty-four."

"No, he doesn't. The picture quality's just bad," Robbie
snapped. I didn't reply. Instead, I began to read the chat log
between my brother and Jimmy.

hockeylover15: I'm seriously going insane.

Jimmy2416: what's wrong??/
hockeylover15: I'm like a slave here. Room might as well be a dungeon.
Jimmy2416: oo kinky ^_~ LOL
hockeylover15: ROFL! OMG, no.
Jimmy2416: sorry couldn't help it.
Jimmy2416: the idea of you in a dungeon . . .
hockeylover15: Awkward.
Jimmy2416: youd like that wouldnt you?
hockeylover2416: Not my thing . . . sorry.
Jimmy2416: im just kidding!!!
Jimmy2416: ::pulls you close and kisses you::
hockeylover2416: =) ::kisses back::

My brother looked up at me. "See? I told you he was nice."

"More like mildly creepy."

"He was joking. Jeez, didn't you see the LOL?"

I said nothing. Something about IM interchange left a bad taste in my mouth as Robbie slipped his cell back in his pocket. Maybe it was the dungeon reference, but Robbie seemed convinced he was joking, and Jimmy *did* use an LOL. I wasn't sure why his being twenty-four bothered me so much either since we were eighteen. It wasn't like the guy was seventy.

We returned to skating, me alongside my brother. I should have been happy that he was smiling, but I kind of felt jealous. Maybe that's what put me on edge—jealousy. I missed Keisha, and unlike *Jimmy,* she was in school right now.

Then Robbie challenged me to a little one-on-one using a rock we found—not that it was any competition—and I forgot about Jimmy. Robbie's talent had always been a source of bitterness, but with the musical, I found I genuinely *wanted* him to get drafted high. Our dreams no longer had to cancel each other out. And if he left, so could I.

I WAS already asleep when Robbie crawled on my mattress and shook me; it was black outside the window. "Tristan, I know how we're going to get out of here," he whispered excitedly. "I know how we're going to get out of this room."

"How?" I asked groggily. Robbie was too close to me. There wasn't enough space. Maybe the room really was shrinking.

"We're going to go live with Jimmy."

I rolled on my side and pulled blankets up over my face.

"No, seriously, hear me out." I reluctantly sat upright and folded my arms over my chest to humor him. Yawning, I blinked my eyes to try and keep awake but I was just so tired. "He lives in Philly. He can drive up, and we'll go out with him, then email Mom and Dad to let them know we're safe, we love them, and are giving them a wake-up call. If they agree to change, we'll go back home right away. If not, we stay with Jimmy until they change their mind, which probably would be another week at the most. Best plan ever, am I right?"

Suddenly, I felt wide awake. I thought about the chat log Robbie let me read. It still unsettled me, maybe more now than it had at the time. "That's sketchy as hell, Robbie. You haven't even met him."

"I *know* him. He's my friend."

"Who hits on you a lot."

"He's not going to do anything. Seriously."

The idea didn't seem that great to me, but Robbie looked thrilled, like he'd thought of the best idea in the world. The last time I saw him look so alive was before he came out, with the guys, on the ice.

"You can see Keisha whenever you want! I bet he'd let you bring her over. Forget bet, I *know* he will."

I stalled with Robbie's obvious bribing. The prospect of

seeing Keisha alone tempted me. It was hard not to think about her. I dreamed about her. I wanted to breathe her.

"Don't you want to be free again? Jimmy's doing us a favor."

The idea didn't seem as bad as it did a few minutes ago. Robbie was a good negotiator. He had some good points. Great ones, even. If Jimmy was some sketchy guy from the net, Robbie would have known by now since they talked for so long online. Whenever we watched the shows on Internet predators, they always went for younger kids anyway, usually girls. We were legal. Jimmy was probably safe.

But this was big. If we ran away and it backfired, we'd be possibly boarded up in the room until draft day. The room would shrink smaller and smaller, until we couldn't move anymore.

What if I told Mom and Dad that Robbie was devising an insane scheme? Maybe they'd send him to a halfway home, or some place where he could be treated. Maybe they'd realize I was the responsible son, and Robbie was being a dumbass and desperately needed help. But why would they take my side? They never had.

Not to mention, if all it took was a few days for our parents to realize the errors of their ways and set us free, that would be worth it. Wouldn't it? My disappearance wouldn't be worth as much as my brother's, but we could have normal lives again. I could get my room back, and spend time with Keisha. He could play hockey.

There would be no backing out once a decision was made. It had to be the right one. Robbie trusted me to make the final call.

I took a deep breath, and decided.

32

obbie refused to speak to me. Not for a week, not even
before the big game, even though I knew how nervous he
was. He'd go out of his way to not look at me at meals, wear
his headphones in the room at all times, texting furiously any
time he wasn't on the computer or doing push-ups or free
weights downstairs. He practiced in the morning with Dad,
leaving me by myself in the room with no company except for
the sound of my tap shoes on the hardwood floor and "Cold
Feets" playing on repeat. In the afternoons, when I'd drive
him to practice, he'd stare out the window.

Really, what did he expect me to do? Running off with
some guy he met online was insane. Sure, people met through
dating sites, but one grainy avatar? Messages not even via text
but AIM?

The day of the big game, Robbie asked Dad to drive him
for morning skate and to just let him stay there so he could
get in game mode, and if he could have fifty dollars for food
just in case.

I counted the minutes between us. I got up and went to
my computer, back to the dolphin story I'd started and never
finished.

They were imprisoned in water, not knowing how to swim despite their appearance and their newly formed gills, which weren't dol-phin-like at all. They were more like sharks. Lungfish. Ones who had feet and didn't know how to swim. They kicked their legs to stay at the top of their tank, taking turns sleeping while the other supported their weight. The survivors kicked and struggled, mouths gaping for breath, not knowing they could breathe with their gills. One of the black beasts began fishing above the tank. The dolphin people strained, tried to resist temptation of the food on the hook. Desperately, one of the dolphin people wrapped his mouth around the jerk bait. The metal pierced through his lower lip. Blood dribbled down his gray chin. He was reeled up, dangling helplessly like an ornament at Christmas.

The other dolphin person, unable to make the top, started to sink beneath the water. Too tired to keep fighting to make the surface, he submitted his soul to the murky depths. He waited for death, but it never came. Just a consistent drowning. He sank lower into the open shell of an oyster, which swallowed him and closed up, then turned into a pearl. The oyster was cracked, the fleshy meat sucked from the shell by the black beasts. The pearl was held in front of the dolphin person, dangling from jerk bait. The captive swallowed the pearl, it disintegrated in his stomach acids, and the dolphin people became one. Their souls fused into one. Their minds one. And when the dolphin person was placed on the chopping block, the black beast's machete glinting as it came down fast; they died together as one.

I SAT next to Dad in the bleachers as the guys spilled onto the ice for warm-ups. They dragged their feet, heads hanging. I scanned for my brother: he wasn't there. My eyes moved to the press box—it was full. One of them was a scout from the Devils. I knew because Dad had mentioned it exactly seventeen times in the past week, and couldn't stop his eyes from darting over there every few minutes.

I got up quickly, scooted away from my parents, muttering, "Bathroom," when Dad frowned. I headed straight for the locker room. Robbie's bag sat outside his stall, still zipped. Next to it was a bag from *Subway*. I peeked inside it—the sub was cold, untouched. The drink next to it was a watery mess. His unopened hockey bag sat right there. Dead weight. I pulled out my phone and texted him: *Where the hell are you?*

Half a minute later, my phone beeped: *nt comming.*

My chest tightened. Robbie would never miss a game. Ever. *Especially* not this game. A no-show from Robbie meant dropping down the draft ratings, or not getting drafted altogether.

But I knew how Robbie had been playing, how his teammates had been treating him. This was my fault. His career was set until he outed himself to protect me. I started this by quitting hockey, and yet, I wouldn't take it back.

When hockey sucked, it had been a fruitless pain. But everything I'd had to endure for the musical was a price that amounted to something. Suffering was worth it, because *this* was what I loved.

And hockey was what Robbie loved.

Of course, I'd seen the cracks, a thousand tiny lines spreading over him as we got deeper into the season. Only one goal after a losing drought. The final game that would determine whether they'd make playoffs or not. I understood why he was hiding from this, but I also knew he'd be heartbroken if he never played hockey again. This game was everything.

I took a deep breath, and rooted through my brother's hockey bag. I changed as quickly as I could into his uniform, which fit, of course. Robbie was a little bigger than me, but with the padding and a helmet covering the non-bleached color of my hair, you couldn't tell. Certainly not from the press box.

I charged through the tunnel and out onto the ice. "Margarine!" Coach snapped from the bench. "You're late!"

He was pissed, but not enough to pull Robbie. That punishment would come later, after Robbie had won them the game. *If* he did.

I skated over to my old teammates. Obviously, helmet or not, I wasn't going to fool them long. Durrell was the first to notice as I fumbled in warm ups with the 2-on-1. "What the hell, Tristan?"

"Butter?" Beau asked, skating up to us. "Is this some sort of joke?"

"Depends on if you think it's funny that your hazing drove my twin away after all the shit he did for you."

Beau reached out to shove me, but I skated just out of reach. "Seriously, how many times was he clutch for you? Playmaker, sniper, two-way forward, faceoff master—whatever you needed."

"Yet he's not here for our most important game," Beau argued.

"Maybe because a stupid game isn't worth his life!"

Beau opened his mouth, but I drove to a hard stop in front of him, ice dusting the front of his skates. "Robbie tried to kill himself."

Beau was silent.

"What did he say?" Durrell asked. Beau gestured for the team to move in. They circled around us, confused.

"Butter," Beau began, "tell them what you just told me."

"Which part?" I snorted. "The part about you guys driving him off a team he's put his soul into for years, or that he tried to kill himself *three times?*"

"He didn't!" Raiden spluttered. "He would have told me."

I looked at Raiden with cold eyes. "From what I understand, he didn't tell you a lot of things, did he?"

Raiden shrunk back. Coward.

I turned in a circle, looking at the guys around me. Over their heads, on the opposite side of the ice, the away team looked at us, shrugging at each other.

"You guys treated him like shit after he came out. Maybe that's why he didn't tell anyone until he felt he had to. Maybe that's why he isn't here at our most important game."

Durrell was the first to speak. "T's right. Robbie saved our asses a few times."

"I don't want to play with some homo," Henry said, nose wrinkling. "He's an abomination of God."

"Fuck you," I snapped. "You think anyone would voluntarily *choose* to be gay with the way you assholes treat them?"

"It's been a distraction," Beau said.

"Because you're making it one! Listen to yourself! Is that the way a team captain should speak?"

The guys were quiet. They glanced at each other, waiting, not wanting to be the one to break the silence.

After a few seconds that felt like hours, Janek said, "I might not understand it fully, but I'm willing to try."

"I don't want him to die," Smitty said. "I don't think any of us do."

"And he's a damn good hockey player," said Ray-Ray.

Henry shook his head. "I don't agree with his life choice. I think it's a sin. And a waste of a draft pick."

"Is it really about religion or you wanting to knock out competition?" I spat.

Silence passed over us. People looked to Beau for an answer.

He finally said, "Why'd you wear Robbie's jersey? You didn't think you'd pass as him, did you?"

My shoulders rounded in. "Maybe he's not here right now, but if he doesn't play, there's no way he's getting drafted. And I know my brother. He loves hockey more than anything. I might suck, but at least he'd be here. At least he could go in a low round."

"We can still save the game," Raiden said, voice almost inaudible. Even though Raiden was just shy of 6'1, he looked so small. "We just need to make Tristan look good. Coach can spread the word that Robbie's sick. Then we do what we can. Get him in the slot, feed him the puck. Sooner or later, it's gotta go in."

"We'll be a wall in front of Janek," Durrell said of the defensemen. "As long as we score, Janek can pull it off."

Beau thought about it, face in a deep grimace. It was down to him, the final vote. He nodded and he touched the C on his jersey. He looked me in the eye. "You stay quick on those damn dancer feet."

"I will," I promised as the buzzer rang. We skated confidently toward the bench. When we got close, Coach narrowed his eyes at me. There was no way he missed our impromptu pow-wow. But he pressed his mouth into a grim line and nodded.

After Beau revved us up in the locker room and we got a last minute pep talk from Coach, Janek bolted onto the ice, followed by Beau. Raiden shoved me out there, pressing me on. "You've got this," he said.

"For Robbie," I said.

"For Robbie," he agreed.

I went up to the face-off circle and got in position.

Crouched, stick poised, ready. It wasn't like I never took a face-off, but I was still scared shitless. As I lifted my head, the ice changed. Lines dotted the ice like a grid in a video game. Angles, spaces. I caught my breath. Felt a harder thud in my chest. Was this what Robbie saw every time he stepped on the ice?

The puck dropped, and my stick snaked out of its own accord. I passed the puck behind me blindly as I raced ahead in a play I was all too familiar with. Within thirty seconds, Beau had a good chance but the goalie blocked it. We skated back to the ice for a line change. Even as I watched from the bench, the grid remained with all its lines and angles. Opportunities.

And suddenly, it was there. I saw it.

I got on my feet, leg already over the boards in preparation of the next line change. The second Henry was over, I was off, cutting off one of their forwards as I stole the puck and forced a turnover. Durrell and Smitty slammed defenders against the wall; the other team hadn't even gotten in range of our goal yet.

The crowd began to make a noise, like a hissing sea. I paid no attention. Everything became white noise. The goalie slipped forward from his crease, glove up, knees bent. I drew my stick up to take a slapshot when I heard a loud, "No."

Robbie.

I felt my body pull to the side, scooping the puck up on the blade and firing it 5-hole.

I didn't even hear the goal horn.

I turned around in a circle, watching the packed arena on their feet screaming. I pounded my fists and did a little boogie the way Robbie always did his celly as my teammates patted me on the helmet and clapped me on the back. I led them back to the bench, fist closed as I bumped all of the players.

"Freaking phenomenal, Margarine," Coach Benoit said

without thinking as he moved me to the front of the bench to take the next shift.

"Butter," I said as I faced him on the bench. "I'm Butter."

Coach gazed at me. A grin broke out on his crooked face. "Butter tastes better."

At the beginning of the second period, I scored again off of one of Raiden's rebounds. I'd never scored a two-goal game in my life.

The third period was more brutal, our opponents gaining momentum as we lost two penalty kills. They tied us up within minutes. As we got closer to the end of the third, and I took each shift, the grid was there but I couldn't see the angles. Like Robbie couldn't see the play.

With a minute to go, I took off, weaving through traffic. Another move presented itself. Risky, not to pass, but it could work. I hesitated—I was moving so fast—but my body careened into the play on its own. Like it was a puppet.

I circled their net, fast, one of their d-men all over me. And, as I twisted, I held onto the puck a second longer than I normally would have. Their goalie went down, falling for the trick. Robbie's trick. I flipped the puck up seconds before their D-man crushed me on the ice and the buzzer sounded. Before I could get up, Raiden was already on top of the guy, yanking him off, spitting, "Get the hell off him!"

My ribs ached as I looked at the referee and stood up. I ignored the pain. There was a hushed silence as I waited for the verdict. Did I beat the clock?

He moved his hands.

Goal.

I screamed.

My scream was swallowed by the crowd as my teammates

launched themselves onto the ice, helmets and gloves flying. Over the glass, a sea of hats rained on me.

We won the game.

I got my first hat trick.

I was practically paraded back to the locker room and barely could get two feet without one of the guys' hugging me or shaking my shoulders with delighted screams. Even in the showers, the guys were screaming.

I took a picture of the pile of collected hats and sent it to Robbie with the text: *Seems like Betterby just got us in the playoffs.*

No answer.

He could be busy, but as my screen stayed continually blank, I realized the twist in my gut was still there. Filling in for Robbie hadn't made it go away. My body was like ice beneath my flushed skin.

Where are you? I texted.

I tried to wait. But didn't. I texted again: *Answer so I know you're okay.*

Nothing.

I called. Straight to voicemail. "I swear to God, if you kill yourself, you fucking coward—" I hung up before finishing my sentence. I didn't sound angry. My voice shook, like I was on the verge of tears.

"Robbie okay?"

I glanced up to see Raiden in front of me, towel around his waist, brow furrowed. I shook my head. "He's not answering my texts. Phone's off."

"Could be blowing off steam if it was as bad as you said it was."

"I guess," I said, though my hand gripped my phone tighter. Raiden didn't leave, shifting uncomfortably, waiting for me to speak. I pulled on a turtleneck. "You know he likes you."

"I don't—"

"You *know* he does."

I waited for Raiden to deny it, to go into some sort of tangent about how it wasn't possible. But he didn't even bother. "I'm straight. I mean, like, really."

"So? That doesn't mean you're immune to feelings."

Raiden was quiet for a few moments. "You know, Robbie was right. You really are chill as hell. I see why he respects you so much." He took a breath. "Do me a favor and tell him to call me later?"

"I will, once I find him."

"Find who?"

We turned as Beau walked out of the showers. Immediately, Raiden's face paled. If Beau had heard anything, his face didn't betray a single hint.

"Robbie's phone's off," I said. "I know he said he wasn't going to the game, but I just want to know where he is."

"I saw him earlier." Beau said. "He came in with his stuff. Was all set, then he got a text. Promised he'd be right back. I think he was trying to get someone into the game to watch."

I froze. ". . . wait, he what? Why didn't you tell anyone?"

"I didn't know he wasn't coming back until you showed up and said all that shit about the suicides and stuff."

I scrolled up through the texts I sent to the last exchange. Before I could stop him, Raiden plucked the phone from my hand. He became rigid.

"That's not Robbie."

"What?" I asked.

"Robbie wouldn't give a two-word answer. He never shuts up, in person *or* in text."

My chest became tight. "Oh my God . . ." I shoved the

rest of Robbie's things into his hockey bag. "I have to find him. Shit."

"You think he's missing?" Raiden asked, voice pinched.

"He's been chatting with this guy online. He wanted to run off with him before. Or maybe he . . . I just—I can feel it, okay? I can feel that something's not right."

"What's going on?" Durrell approached.

"I gotta go." I grabbed Robbie's bag and slung it over my shoulder.

"We'll look for him," Raiden blurted. He glanced at Durrell, then Beau. "Right? Tristan thinks Robbie's missing. Like maybe he's in trouble, or . . . he's hurt himself."

Durrell frowned. "We'll look," he said. "We'll all look, block off areas. Whatever else has happened, he's still our teammate."

Robbie would be pissed as hell once he found out I told them about the suicides, but I didn't care. If he was pissed, that meant he was alive. "Text me if you find anything. Thanks." I didn't wait for a reply as I ran out, Robbie's bag over my back.

My parents were waiting near the locker room doors as the crowds filed out. At first glance, Dad grinned when he saw me, but soon that faded.

"Tristan?" he asked as he walked close. "What are you doing with Robbie's stuff?"

I slowed. "He's missing."

"What do you mean?"

Now or never. "He's missing. I took his place on the ice. Only realized when I got back that he was gone for real."

I waited for the inevitable. The freak out, the excuses, the everything. But instead, Dad said the words I needed to hear: "We have to go to the police."

33

I wasn't sure what I was looking for as I rummaged through Robbie's room. Downstairs, Dad was yelling at the police on the phone. Robbie was eighteen and he sent a text that said he wasn't coming. The cops wouldn't do anything for at least seventy-two hours. I tried to tune out the noise as I looked through Robbie's things. There was nothing in the pile of clothes, the mattress. Nothing usual. Even the piece of paper he kept under his pillow with the phone calls from NHL teams was there, untouched.

I looked at his computer. He'd kill me. He'd absolutely *kill* me.

But someone went to see Robbie play.

And Robbie didn't play.

I booted up the computer and looked around his hard drive but I didn't find anything. Then I logged in to his Facebook using the password: *margarine16*. Nothing on his timeline.

I clicked on the messages, and my blood went cold.

There were thousands of messages with Jimmy—including details of the game, Robbie promising he'd win for Jimmy. He wouldn't have time to hang out before, but would get him the seat, and afterward he'd get an excuse so they could hang out, alone.

There was a link to something on Google Drive. I clicked

on it. It was password protected. It was a long shot that some-one would have the same password for both, but I typed in *margarine16* anyway.

Immediately, I wished I hadn't.

There were pictures. So many pictures, mostly taken in our bathroom. Robbie with the fake piercing, sticking his tongue out. Robbie without his shirt, flexing his muscles. Dick pics. A video I was smart enough not to play.

Downstairs, my parents had started arguing with each other instead. I pulled out my cell and sent a text to Durrell. *On my way.*

An immediate response, *Find anything?*

I hesitated as I looked at the computer, then typed back. *Yeah. Tell you when I get there.*

I jogged downstairs. Dad sat on the couch with his head in his hands. Mom looked up at me, eyes glassy and dazed.

"I'm looking for him," I said, answering her unasked ques-tion. "All of the guys on the team are. He said something about Philly before, so I thought maybe I'd look around there." I'd watched enough crime shows to know that the first forty-eight hours were the most crucial in finding a missing person or solving a crime. Seventy-two hours might be too late.

Dad didn't ask me how I knew. "Lynn, you stay here in case Robbie comes home. Call if anything happens." He stood and nodded. "I'll follow behind you. We'll cover more ground if we drive separate."

If it were any other time, it would have been almost warm. In the midst of tragedy, we were becoming a family.

34

O f course, it had to snow.

The windshield wipers on my old car flapped against the slush as I drove on at a crawling pace. The entire team, Dad, even Keisha and Craig, were out looking for Robbie. Going through Robbie and Jimmy's messages, there were definitely references to Philadelphia, but Philly was huge. It was a long shot that we'd find him, but we had nothing else to go on.

Durrell divided everyone up in different zones. The underclassmen on the hockey team, who didn't have their licenses, stayed local and asked around in case anyone who would recognize Robbie had seen him. The rest of us had cars, and we figured we'd cover more ground driving separately.

I was on the outskirts of the city, about a half-hour into Pennsylvania. I hadn't actually seen a house in over a mile. Nothing there really, just a few bare trees straining in the oncoming storm. I was pushed forward by nothing more than gut feeling. My phone was nearly dead thanks to the constant stream of relayed calls, and I was getting low on gas too, but I couldn't turn around yet. I had to find Robbie. I felt, maybe irrationally, that I was the only one who *could* find him.

The wind gusted hard and my hands jerked on the wheel, causing the tires to briefly catch and slide along the fresh snow. I squeezed the wheel as the car came to a stop, took a deep breath, then squinted into the glare of my headlights. There, almost completely hidden by trees, was a path. And suddenly, in my head, a vision.

I was moving. Floating. Outside of my body, I walked ahead, seeing through someone's eyes. I tried to look to the side but couldn't. My path was straight.

". . . are you Jimmy?"

I recognized my brother's voice, but it came from my lips.

I was barely conscious of turning my car off and stepping out, ignoring the snow that collected around my boots. *Robbie.*

He was alive.

Using my iPhone as a light, I walked down the path, tripping through the snow, not sure where I was going, but sure I was going the right way.

"Robbie! I'm so thrilled to meet you."

I stepped back. Robbie's hand—my hand?—drew back and tucked into his side. "You don't look anything like your picture."

"And you look a hell of a lot older than fifteen."

"I told you, I'm eighteen."

I kept my head low as I forced myself forward. In the distance, there was a broken-down house. I picked up my pace, ignoring my chattering teeth. The light on my phone used the last of its battery and I had to stumble the rest of the way in the dark. I walked up to the house, wondering if I should knock when that pull came again, tugging me around to the side. I peered in through a window—everything was dark. I pressed against it and it slid open. With a grunt and hop, I had the sill under my arms and forced my way through. The second my feet touched ground, there was warmth.

I closed my eyes. Come on, Robbie. Where are you?

"Your profile seemed like a kid's. I thought you were just lying to use a site like that."

"The hell? That's sick."

I went up the stairs, not sure whether to creep or speed up. At the top, there was only one room. Its door was closed. I pulled it open and staggered back.

My brother was on the floor, tied up. A gag was forced into his mouth. His face was bruised, a little cut up. Through his lip where he normally wore his fake piercing was a piece of jerk bait, blood dried around the hole where the hook was forced in.

I dove on the floor and tore at the knots on his legs first. My brother made some sort of muted cry and I lifted my head. His eyes widened, fixed on something over my shoulder. Before I could turn, it crashed down hard on my head, sending me face down on the floor.

"I think you should leave." My vision shook as Robbie turned. He *didn't get far before his body lit up. A searing pain by his side. My side. A brief paralysis.*

A taser.

The man leaned down. In our ear, he whispered, "Get in the fucking car."

And everything went black.

35

*T*ristan.

I floated over rooftops. I saw the houses below, the streets, the snow on the ground. Ice. It was so cold. Goosebumps broke out over my body. Sweat was thick, slick on my back, slipping down my spine.

Tristan!

Something was tugging me down to Earth. It clung to my wrists, my ankles. Slithered around like snakes. Living shackles. I was too tired to fight the pull of gravity. Submitted to some sort of unknown.

Tristan! Tristan! Oh God, Tristan, please wake up.

A distant light ship. Lightning on the bay. Sinking into the sea where the dolphin people were. Deeper, deeper, a dolphin person above me attached to a piece of jerkbait. Deeper, deeper, as I was sucked into the open mouth of an oyster. But that wasn't right. That couldn't have been right.

Tristan! Tristan!

The ocean disappeared around me. Fat raindrops landed on my face. An earthquake. No, a tsunami.

Tristan! Tristan! Wake the hell up or I swear to God I'll beat your face in!

I blinked opened my eyes. They stung from salt. My mouth was sore by the corners. I tried to move, but my body wouldn't.

Tristan! Please wake up! PLEASE!

I turned my head, blurry eyes slowly adjusting. The room pulsed: *dark, light, dark, light, light, dark, dark, dark.* The first thing that came into focus was my brother, sitting next to me, gagged and tied with rope, hand barely able to grip mine, but soon that blurred too, like I was watching him through a heat wave in the desert.

I lowered my head and tried to move. I was tied up, just like him. Gagged as well. My heavy winter coat was gone.

What happened? I thought, shivering.

He knocked you out, I heard Robbie in my head. *I should have listened to you about not meeting Jimmy. I'm so fucking stupid.*

How did he get you?

Tears slid down Robbie's cheeks, mixing with dried blood on his chin. *Taser.*

My heart rate sped up. *Before the game?*

My twin looked surprised. *How did you—?*

I saw it. I'm not sure how. But I saw it.

My body and mind still felt separated, brain wanting to float away, like a helium balloon trapped in my skull. I saw the black beasts whacking the heads off of the dolphin people with machetes.

I strained to turn so I could see Robbie better. My limbs were too heavy, the rope painfully cutting into my flesh. My twin became limp against the restraints. *We're going to die, aren't we?*

I pressed my side against his. Robbie felt small, too small for an athlete, too small to truly defend either of us. There was nothing to say. We had to fight our way out, but as I twisted so my back was to his, my fingers couldn't get a good hold on his restraints. I was too weak.

Squinting as if it would clear my vision, I looked around

the room. There was one window, but who knew what was below the drop. Concrete, snow? No curtains—just venetian blinds blocking gray daylight. There were two closed doors—which was the way out?—and a bed that had just a thin, worn sheet on it. Next to it was a wood chest.

Gritting my teeth around the gag, I forced myself over, wriggling to get across the floor. My body was exhausted, the pace excruciatingly slow.

What are you doing? Robbie asked, watching as I twisted so my back was to the wood chest's front. With a few grunts and heaves, I worked the top open and peered in. Immediately, I wished I hadn't. Restraints, sex toys, a video camera. Nothing that could be used to get out.

I sank down, letting the top slam down with a frustrated bang.

"What was that?" The ferocious voice came from below the floor, matching the one I heard in Robbie's memory. *Jimmy.* Tense, I tried to wriggle back across the floor. Robbie made a muffled cry around his gag as footsteps thudded up the stairs. The lock turned, door swinging in with me halfway to my brother.

My body lost its ability to move. Paralyzed with fear, I watched as a lanky man walked across the floor and loomed directly above me. He pressed his boot between my shoulders and I flattened out on the ground.

"You're more behaved than him, aren't you?" Jimmy asked.

I didn't make a sound. Not even a whimper. My body didn't budge. A few feet away from us, my brother trembled with a fear that was slowly turning to anger.

Good. An angry Robbie was a force to be reckoned with. There had to be a way to use that sort of rage to our advantage—I just wasn't sure how.

Jimmy dropped to a squat, his boot still between my shoulder blades. "Robbie never told me he had a twin. So now, I need to figure out what I'm going to do with both of you."

I remained still. Allowed Jimmy's words to slide over me. He dug his toe in my back, looking for a response. Fear, or a fight. I refused to give in.

The pressure on my back alleviated as Jimmy stood. He pulled his leg back and his boot connected with my ribs. I gasped, body coiling involuntarily. From the corner of my eye, I saw Jimmy's lips curled up in a smile as he strode to the door. He stepped out and closed it behind him. We heard the twist of the lock, then the thuds of Jimmy going down the steps.

Robbie twisted his body, scooting across the ground until he was behind me. Back to mine, his fingers felt for the ends of my restraints. I had been too weak, but Robbie—fueled by the same furious determination I'd seen the day he defended me in the lunchroom—was not. Despite the pain, I tried to do the same, our hands sometimes brushing as we grabbed what we could. Finally, the rope around Robbie's arms gave free. Before undoing his legs, he faced my back and worked on my arms, yanking the knots until there was just enough slack for me to get out. We noiselessly worked on our legs and, finally, the gags.

Freed from restraint, we rested our heads together, breathing heavily, aching and stiff. I looked around the room once more, taking inventory of everything from the bed to the trunk, to the loose rope on the floor, and the window. There was a way out. It was in the corner of my brain, fuzzy and unfocused.

I staggered to my feet and walked to the window before pulling up the blinds and peering down. Second story window into snow. Last night's storm had left a morning of deep snow. Not deep enough to prevent a fall, but . . .

This was our way out.

Help me move the trunk, I thought to my brother. We lifted it together, carrying it to the window as quietly as we could. We wrapped and knotted the rope around it, pressing it to the wall below the window. Robbie's shaking fingers curled around the edge of the glass pane. With a careful nudge, the window creaked and slid open.

We threw the ropes over the side before looking down. My face fell. There was no way the trunk and rope would hold both of our weights. But, before I could think of another idea, Robbie pushed me to the window. *Hold the rope, then my hands.*

I bit the inside of my cheek before carefully crawling through the window, hanging onto the rope with both hands. Robbie leaned out the window, gripping my forearms for support as he folded his torso over. Even with our stretched out heights, the drop was still at least six feet. I took a deep breath and let go, trying to keep my knees bent to absorb the shock. Pain seared up my legs, but adrenaline had me on my feet again, arms stretched up for my brother. He gazed down at me, lips in a firm line as he studied the distance. In my head, I could hear him calculating the drop, how far he'd have before I'd catch him.

Hurry up!

His frown deepened—and finally I understood his hesitation. If I didn't break Robbie's fall, he could break a leg, his femur. His career could be over.

It's not worth your life! I desperately thought.

Robbie shook his head. *Get help.*

I'm not leaving you.

I'll find another way. Get help.

I trembled, calf-deep in the snow, not wanting to leave, but knowing my brother wouldn't budge. I could rush inside again, possibly getting myself and Robbie killed, or I could run through the woods, back to my car, and try to find a gas station or anywhere with a phone. But, by then, Jimmy would certainly discover I was missing. He wouldn't be forgiving, and Robbie would bear the brunt of his sadism alone.

My brother's head snapped away from the window, hearing something I couldn't. Jimmy on the stairs? Jimmy in the room?

I had to make a decision, and fast.

36

My heartbeat thudded in my ears. It barely drowned out the profanities my brother mentally spewed as I crept around the house, looking for something—a large branch, firewood, anything—that I could use as a weapon. Barreling in through the front door wasn't exactly a good plan, but like hell was I leaving Robbie behind.

My options for weapons were limited in the frosty world. I closed my hands around a tree branch in the nearby woods, shuddering as a sheet of snow dumped on me. I could barely feel my fingers. Gritting my teeth didn't do much—the branch didn't snap. It bent, mocking me.

Suddenly, my chest seized, clenching and pulsing around my heart in pain. My blood became as cold as the snow. I took off toward the front door of the house with no weapon except my fists.

The clenching came faster, moving down my ribs to my side the closer I came to the front door. I gripped the doorknob and heard a series of thuds and yells, like something slamming against a wall or floor.

The room turned on its side. Fists—Robbie's fists, our fists—connected with Jimmy's jaw. "You son of a bitch!" Robbie's voice erupted from my lips, hands twisting around Jimmy's shoulders, throwing him against the wall with our strength. There was a cracking of bone and blood. Jimmy swearing and groping in his pocket for something. A taser. Robbie's vision—my vision—shifted toward the window. It was ahead of him—us—our freedom right there. I urged him forward but his dream of becoming an NHL superstar was holding him back. Jimmy lurched towards us. There was no choice. We sprinted toward it.

My vision—Robbie's vision—went black. Then I heard it. An inhuman scream, a loud thud. My heart pounded, throat tight in realization:

Robbie jumped.

Without me to break his fall.

I raced around the side of the house to the window, fully prepared to see my brother running toward me, screaming at me to go. What I saw stopped me dead in my tracks.

". . . no," I whispered.

The snow surrounding the body was turning red, soaking in blood. Face down, hoodie swallowing him whole. Unbudging. Unconscious. Broken.

Shakily, I took a step toward him, then another, and another. Tears streaked down my cheeks as I stood over his body, afraid to touch him. Why had I climbed out of the window before him? Why couldn't Robbie have gone first, or trusted that I would have caught him, breaking his fall?

I sank to my knees in the deep snow, which came up well over my thighs. My hand closed on his shoulder, then I realized what was wrong:

His breath wasn't fogging in the frigid snow, because there was no breath.

"No. No, no, no—" I choked. I'd tried so hard to put the pieces of Robbie together when the seams came undone, but in the end I failed him. He'd leapt for freedom, leapt to save his life.

He ended up broken.

Mangled.

Dead.

With a deep breath, I gripped his shoulders and rolled him onto his back.

Immediately, I recoiled, scrambling backward in the snow. A scream stuck in my paralyzed throat; Jimmy's battered face stared back at me. His eyes were still open. Dead.

Then my screams came, one after another, and another, so loud and hoarse I couldn't process the muffled footsteps in the snow. I didn't budge as Robbie knelt next to me, arms wrapping around me, turning my face into his shoulder as if to protect me. His chin pressed on top of my head, the rusted piece of jerkbait through his lip by my ear as he said, "I told you I'd find another way out," and it was so absurd my sobs turned to laughter. Laughter that he joined in with.

We sounded identical, our hearts, our breath synchronized. Identical lungs, identical body, with two vastly different minds. Two people, once strangers.

As I shivered, body slowing down, Robbie asked, "Where'd you come from? When you found me, I mean."

I studied our surroundings, trying to find the snowy trail I'd come in from, but there seemed to be three, and my mind was slowly numbing. With the heavy snow and strong wind, my tracks were covered. The clouds were too thick to make out the sun, but it was cold enough to be early morning. We had time to find the right one before it got dark again.

I closed my eyes as if it'd help me sense whatever direction we should travel in, but I wasn't sure. My brain was too fatigued to work. I looked at the house, wondering if we could temporarily get shelter, maybe find a phone. Or at least my coat since I didn't have a heavy hoodie like Robbie. I wasn't even sure why Jimmy took mine. But, before I could speak, he said, "I can't go back in there. I just . . . can't."

Staring at the jerkbait in his lip, I didn't even attempt to change his mind. I didn't see the torture he must have experienced. "I don't think I walked far. I'm sure we'll run into my car eventually." I tried to sound confident. "You want to pick a trail?"

Robbie looked between the three and chose the one in the center. No surprise there. We crunched through the snow, my body barely moving. We hadn't even started, and it was already hard to keep my head up. It was so cold, and every part of me felt so, so heavy.

We dragged our feet, stumbling in the snow, slipping in the cold. Now, more than ever, I wanted to go home, to *be* home, whatever that meant. I didn't even care if we never got to leave our room again.

We continued to trudge through the calf-deep snow and slush that soaked through my jeans. The woods seemed much bigger than they had last night. The heavy clouds turned the sun's glow into a dark, shadowy mess. The storm was rolling back, stronger and crueler. The wind whipped snow up in our faces, bending the trees.

Beside me, Robbie kept stopping, taking long, careful steps; I almost told him to hurry up, until I realized he was keeping his pace slow enough to match mine.

"Is it bad that I don't feel bad about shoving him out the window?" Robbie asked, breaking the silence.

"I don't think so. I mean, self-defense, right?"

"Right." My brother's pace slowed even further as I gritted my teeth and tried to press faster. But each step became harder and harder to take. How long had we been walking?

It felt like hours. "He didn't kiss me," Robbie continued. "So that's something, right? I mean, at least I could still have a first kiss, you know?"

"You've never been kissed?" I gawked. "How? I mean, you're . . . popular. I'd have thought you would have kissed a few girls or something."

"Why would I want to do that?" Robbie asked, wrinkling his red nose. "It's not like I was confused. I've known since I was seven." He rubbed his arms. "Jimmy was supposed to be my first everything."

I hesitated, not wanting to ask the question I knew I had to. "What did he do?"

Robbie refused to look me in the eye. "You know."

My stomach sank to my feet.

Robbie tried to kick up some snow but it was too deep. "I'm not sure whether I want to avoid touching anyone for the rest of my life or sleep with a guy as soon as possible to forget this . . . stuff. Is that weird?"

"I d-don't know," I said, tongue slurring in the cold. "I'd read s-stuff about skin cells getting replaced every s-seven years."

"Every seven?"

I licked my lips, talking through my teeth to stop the chattering. "If it's t-true, that means when you're twenty-five, it'd be almost like you're new. And I mean, you've still got that first kiss, right? Maybe Raiden could d-do the honors."

Robbie snorted. "Yeah, right. He hates me."

"No, he d-doesn't," I paused, not sure how to continue. This wasn't my confession to make. Raiden could talk to Robbie himself, because we were both going to get out of these woods, both going to be fine. I hugged my arms around myself and forced my next few steps to be faster. "Just . . . t-trust me. Okay?"

"What are you trying to say?" Robbie asked warily. "Did you talk about me?"

I opened my mouth to speak, but my foot caught on a tree root hidden by snow. I hit the ground and broke into shivering spasms. Robbie's arms wrapped around me, holding me up. "The hell?"

Again, I tried to speak, to tell him I was fine, but my lips wouldn't stop shaking long enough to work. Harsh buzzing rushed into my head. My legs wouldn't move despite me commanding them to.

"No. No, no, no, Tristan, no," I heard Robbie say, but his voice was faint and far away. So much easier to close my eyes. I just needed a minute, and I'd get up.

I snapped back into consciousness, unaware I'd drifted off. Robbie had hoisted me over his back. My body felt weightless dangling over his shoulder. After a minute, I realized he'd turned around, back toward the house he so desperately wanted to get away from.

With the heavy wind and his fatigue, it seemed like Robbie was barely moving as he carried me, body pitched forward with determination. I squinted, catching something from the corner of my eye. To our right, a flickering glow. *There*, I pointed.

Robbie turned. Like a moth, he was drawn to the light. He paused when it moved again. Someone held a flashlight. I wondered if it was Jimmy, somehow not-dead, or one of Jimmy's friends, and by the way Robbie sucked back, I could tell he was thinking the same. But he broke into a run, crashing through the branches and snow as he screamed, "HELP!"

The light flashed again in our direction, blinding me.

Robbie pressed on, screaming "Help!" until his voice was hoarse and the flashlight and figure behind it came crashing toward us. I screamed as heavy arms wrapped around us, trying to pull away before I heard a familiar voice: "Oh my God. Thank God, thank fucking God."

Dad.

There was something calm about identifying him. That he'd come out looking. How had he found us? My eyelids became heavier. My body was lifted, moving from Robbie's arms to Dad's. I couldn't keep my head up as I closed my eyes.

Robbie was safe. We were safe.

37

I came to in a dimly-lit white room. The pillowcase was thin and scratchy. I blinked a few times before trying to sit upright. My eyes focused on my arm and the IV sticking out of it.

"You're awake."

I turned my head to the side, focusing on Robbie. He sat on the bed. There were a couple of black stitches on his lower lip from where Jimmy forced in the fishhook.

"How are you feeling?"

"Like shit," I said, groaning a little. "What happened?"

"You passed out. Hypothermia. Fortunately, Dad and the cops found your car and were there looking. Wasn't long before the ambulance got there."

"Huh? How?"

"GPS on the iPhone. Even though it died, they were able to pinpoint a general location. When you disappeared, I guess it was enough of a viable threat for the police to take it seriously. At least serious enough to break the seventy-two-hour window."

I could barely nod, let alone keep my eyelids open. "How are you?" I asked, voice a little gravelly.

"Better, since you're okay." He looked at the wall. "They did a rape kit. Not sure why since the bastard's dead but I guess when it goes to trial—"

That wasn't what I was expecting to hear. "It's going to trial?"

"It has to." Robbie lay next to me on the bed. "Always goes to trial if a death's involved."

"I'm sorry."

"Yeah. Me, too." He forced a smile, but it didn't seem sincere. "But hey, now I can get therapy. First appointment is in two days."

"That's good. That you're getting help, you know."

"I know." Robbie looked away; he didn't sound glad, he sounded tired. "If it makes you feel better, I think I'm going to commit to a team in juniors."

"Yeah?" I perked up through my fuzzy tiredness, even if he'd couched the news as something that would make *me* feel better.

"If it wasn't too late and I was smart enough, I'd maybe see about college hockey. You know, Raiden's going to Providence. With the way he texts, I'd never believe it."

"I'm sure it wouldn't be too late for you to apply. I mean, pretty sure a LOT of colleges would want someone like you on their team."

"It's not for me, Tristan," Robbie said. "I can always do classes online, if I wanted. Or when I'm done with my career . . ." He suddenly shook his head, like snapping out of a reverie. "I don't know why I'm even talking like this. No one's going to draft me this year with a pending trial. Maybe ever."

Before I could speak, there was a knock at the door. Mom slipped in. Her immaculate red fingernails were now plain and chipped. Without make up, she looked older and wearier, but somehow more human. More like a parent.

She looked at me before crossing the room, sitting on the

side of the bed opposite of Robbie, and embracing me tightly. I rested my head against her shoulder.

"I'm so sorry," Mom said. "I'm so . . . so sorry."

"It's okay," I began.

"No. It's not okay. At all." She squeezed me tighter. "You don't need to forgive me, and I'm not sure I can make it right, but I'm going to try to be better." She inhaled slowly. "I want to see you in your musical."

"Really?"

"I do. Your Uncle Anthony would have been thrilled to find out one of his nephews was into acting."

I was unaware of the tears until Mom squeezed me tighter and wiped my cheeks. The first recognition gave way, like something toppling. Sniffing back couldn't keep me from bawling for the eighteen years of being starved for affection, touch, recognition.

I cried straight into sleep. When I woke up, I wondered if I'd dreamed it, but Mom was still sitting on the corner of my bed, one of her hands around mine, reading a book. Her iPhone was out of sight.

I squeezed her hand as I sat upright, and Mom set down her book. "Did you rest well?" she asked.

"I think," I said, my voice a little less gravelly than it had been. "I can feel my toes."

"Good."

I looked around the room. "Where's Robbie?"

Mom hesitated and glanced toward her purse, probably where her cell was. "He and your father should be back any minute."

"Okay, but where are they?"

Mom didn't answer. My cheeks started to burn. "For fuck's

sake, they're not doing stupid draft shit right now after all this, are they?"

"You really suck with surprises," my brother's voice came into the room, a tinge of amusement in his tone rather than annoyance. When I turned to the door to face him, I saw not only my brother and Dad, but Keisha. The heaviness on my chest lifted, and my cheeks burned from embarrassment.

"You're welcome," Robbie said before slipping out of the room.

Keisha hesitated before coming in, a plastic bag in hand, Dad right behind her. Before approaching me, she went directly to my mother and held out her hand.

"It's really nice to meet you, Mrs. Betterby. I'm Keisha Lewis. I take acting class with Tristan and—"

"She's his girlfriend," Dad said.

"I know who Keisha is. Tristan showed me her picture." Mom rose to her feet. Instead of taking her hand, she pulled Keisha into a tight hug. "I thought Tristan was exaggerating when he said how beautiful you are. I was wrong."

"That's so sweet." Keisha squeezed Mom and pulled back beaming. "I hope you don't mind that I brought some stuff over," she said as she rooted through the plastic bag and pulled out a few Tupperware containers with different foods and sweets. "My grandma's visiting from Trinidad and made us some Callaloo with some plantain and sweet potatoes, and there's some jerk chicken, so I brought over the leftovers. The brownies and cookies were just box stuff. Unfortunately, my cooking skills are inherited from my dad."

I stared at Keisha. She was absolutely captivating. And judging by the rare smiles on my parents' faces, she was winning them over without even trying.

"You probably want to spend some time with Tristan," Mom said as she gestured to the chair she was sitting in. She set the Tupperware containers on another empty chair. "We'll give you two some privacy."

"Just let me know when you need a lift home," Dad said to Keisha before he and Mom left the room.

"Unfortunately I don't think I'll be able to stay much more than a half-hour since Grandma's over and I've got a huge test tomorrow," Keisha said, face a little down. "But if it's all right, I'd love to visit tomorrow."

"I'm hoping I'll be home by tomorrow," I said.

"Even better."

Keisha leaned over the bed and kissed me. "I was so scared when you went off the grid looking for Robbie. Then when Robbie showed up with your Dad saying you were at the hospital, I just . . . I don't know what I imagined."

"Probably more gruesome than hypothermia."

"That's pretty gruesome itself, though."

"Robbie had it way worse."

"This isn't a pissing contest," Keisha said. "I can still worry about you *and* fuss over you even if your brother *did* have it worse. It just means I have an excuse to make more cookies, even if they're kind of inedible."

I reached for the back of Keisha's neck and gently pulled her down for a second kiss. "You're right. I just still feel awful about Robbie."

"Of course, you do. He's your twin." She opened a Tupperware container and pulled out a chocolate chip cookie for me. It was pretty burned, but still tasted like the best thing ever.

"You're sure you can't stay longer?" I asked, hand on her hip.

"Not unless you take my test for me and can guarantee I'll get at least ninety-three percent."

"What subject?"

"Biochemistry."

"Oh, dear God." We both started to laugh, like it was our own stupid joke even though it wasn't exactly a joke, or funny. Keisha left with my parents, having stretched her half-hour limit to nearly an hour, and I realized I hadn't seen Robbie since he dropped her off. I grabbed my cell from the table next to my hospital bed, noticed it was fully charged, and hesitated before I sent him a short text: *Thanks.*

Seconds later, his reply: *You're welcome. Give me a lift to therapy?*

I smiled.

You bet.

38

Our rooms looked almost normal. Mine still had a patch in the ceiling where the fan was, and the bunk bed was still there. The window in Robbie's was still sealed shut. The desks were returned, along with our computers. Even the staplers.

I turned over on the bottom bunk. I finally had my room to myself again, and suddenly it felt too big. Was it possible to get claustrophobic in reverse? This was our first night at home since Jimmy's, and I wasn't afraid, exactly, just . . .

Okay.

A little afraid. Jimmy's dead face. Red on the white snow.

I pulled the sheets over my shoulders. Stuffed them back down a minute later. I sighed and heard, *Can't sleep either?* in my head.

I turned. Robbie stood in the shadow of my doorway, silently closing the door behind him. He didn't say a word as he moved to the edge of my bed. I scooted over and lifted the covers. He climbed in beside me and we shifted around, attempting to fit both of us on the single mattress, which was only mildly successful. Robbie muttered something about me taking it easy on the Twinkies. We shook with silent laughter, side by side, long enough to know it was about more than Twinkies. "Tomorrow," Robbie whispered, "I'll take the top bunk."

Tomorrow.

I sighed. We drifted into silence, our breaths syncing. "Are you going to call any of those groups?"

I'd driven Robbie to his first therapy session today and he'd come out armed with pamphlets for organizations like You Can Play and The Trevor Project. He hadn't exactly been enthusiastic about them.

"I'm not sure they're for me," he muttered.

"Um, one's for gay athletes." You Can Play was perfect for my brother, and we'd all seen the NHL commercials, different players stating their acceptance and welcoming of LGBT athletes in professional sports. "Of course, they're for you."

"Yeah, but . . ." Robbie's voice trailed off. "It doesn't matter. Not like they're going to do anything. Probably shouldn't even bother with therapy."

"You were looking forward to it."

"Yeah, but I don't feel any better."

"You had *one* session. It's not an overnight thing."

"How would you know? You've never gone."

I said nothing, and took my own advice. *It's not an overnight thing.*

I needed to do something to help. I wasn't sure what I could do that would make a difference, but I was no longer willing to sit back, passively, waiting for something to happen. As much as I wanted to be my brother's anchor, I knew I couldn't be the only one helping him. He needed a whole support system.

And maybe that was why I dug out my cell and sent the text.

39

I skated next to Robbie at the pond. We wore our gloves and carried sticks, passing a puck between us. It was the only way I could get him to say yes to going out. It hadn't been a full week, but Robbie wasn't getting better. He was getting worse, the light in his eyes dimmer, his desire emptier.

"Did you call any of those groups?" I asked as we cut across the ice to change direction, flipping the puck on my stick like a pancake. Before it could reconnect with the tape on my stick, Robbie's stick snaked above mine and stole the puck.

"No."

"This afternoon, then?"

"Lay off it," Robbie said firmly, picking up the pace in a silent challenge for a one-on-one. I hustled to catch up to him. I only made a few laps before I stopped, hands pressed on my thighs, panting.

"You okay?" Robbie asked, stopping before me.

I nodded before getting out a yes. I stood upright as a car pulled up to the edge of the pond next to mine.

With the sun's glare on the snow, I could make out the shadowed outline the figure getting out of the driver's side, rooting in the backseat for gear. I held my breath as I looked at Robbie, who was stock still, then back to the figure leaving the car, picking his way on the ice carefully before pushing off and skating toward my brother.

I kept a close distance. Robbie didn't move until Raiden faced us.

"The hell do you want?" Robbie asked, tone sharper than I thought it would be. My chest tightened—what if I screwed up again? What if texting Raiden was the last thing Robbie needed, not the thing he needed most?

I'd never seen Raiden so silent around my brother. He didn't utter a word, not a snarky comment or a stupid joke. Not even a quote from *Happy Gilmore*.

"I said, what do you want?" Robbie growled. He drew up his stick in both hands, shoving it against Raiden's chest to push him back on the ice. A show of assertion in the hockey world. A statement if a referee made the wrong call.

I guess I was the referee. And judging by Robbie's stance, I made the wrong call. Or text, rather.

Raiden took a step back, and Robbie used his stick to give him another hard shove. That time, instinct kicked in and Raiden pushed Robbie, hard. Before I could blink, their sticks and gloves were on the ice. Robbie lunged toward Raiden. They gripped each other's collars, holding each other at a distance as they swung, sometimes catching part of the other's jaw with their bare knuckles. Their bodies careened from side-to-side until they toppled to the ground, Raiden on top of my brother. Robbie's body became limp as he released his hold on Raiden's coat and covered his face. I could hear his muffled cries.

Before I could skate forward to assess the situation, Raiden got to his knees. Straddled over my brother, he pried Robbie's hands away from his face and leaned down, whispering something I couldn't hear. He rested his forehead against Robbie's, murmuring something again. His shoulders quaked, then his head dropped, closing the gap between them as he kissed my twin, long, careful, and slow.

I watched them on the ice, kissing under the morning sun. No one else in the world but them. When my brother's arms wrapped around Raiden's shoulders, I took my cue.

I skated off the ice as silently as I could, started my car, and backed out of the parking lot.

On the highway, I flickered on the lights as I drove home solo in the morning snow. Raiden couldn't cure my brother's depression, but he could help give him the strength to keep going, keep trying to get help. As I parked my car, sun broke through the heavy clouds. Peeking through the snow were a dozen crocus buds. The end of our winter gave way to hope, and I'd never felt so light, so connected, so strong.

EPILOGUE

I stood in the wings waiting for "Cold Feets." Opening night. I was floating; I was where I belonged. There was no nausea, no pounding heart, no constriction around my throat. There was nothing to be afraid of when nothing could match what I felt the night Robbie was taken, or Jimmy's dead body in the snow.

From the wings, I scanned the audience as Heather belted out "Show Off." Really, it was a perfect role for her. I could admit that even though we'd refused to talk outside of rehearsal, only interacting for our numbers. It almost wasn't fair that she hadn't paid for what she did, but I guess that's showbiz.

My eyes sorted through the crowd. Mom and Dad were in the first row, dead center. Before I could find my brother, I was tapped on the shoulder by Cade, the guy playing George.

I nodded and slipped to the side of the stage, waiting for my cue. As soon as the stage darkened just enough, the atten tion on the Man in Chair, I slipped behind an open frame that was supposed to be a mirror. The second I came into full sight, pulling into my toothpaste commercial grin, the theatre erupted so loudly, the Man in Chair had to pause before his monologue. As my eyes adjusted to the bright lights, I could make out not only my parents in the first row, but the hockey team taking up the next few rows near them, screaming and hollering their support. Robbie was welcomed back to the team and basically won them the playoffs, but he gave me his trophy, saying it was really mine. He sat by Raiden, smiling and whispering something in his ear. Their hands were beneath the armrest that separated them. I imagined their pinkies were linked.

I slipped into "Cold Feets," spurred by the crowd's energy. I tapped clean and quick, not faltering on the tricky steps as Cade joined me for our short duet. We finished to thunderous applause.

I WAS ready to leave the theatre with Keisha when a voice drew my attention.

"Tristan."

Without looking, I knew who it was. So did Keisha.

"I'll catch you outside. Tell my parents I'll be out in a few," I told Keisha, giving her a quick kiss before I turned back. I shoved my hands in my pockets and walked backstage. "What do you want?"

Heather stood hugging her sides, trying to force eye contact. "Just thought we should talk."

"Oh, really? Because I got more applause than you?"

Heather twitched. "Just thought you should know that Durrell and I aren't a couple anymore."

"What a shocker."

"He broke up with me."

"*Shocker.*"

"Tristan, don't," Heather said in that tone that used to make me crumble. I pursed my lips together so I wouldn't fall back into my old habits of apology. She continued, "I wish I could give you a good reason as to why I did what I did. I just . . . I messed up. Big time." She looked me in the eye, biting her lip. Heather was a good actor, but I'd helped her with enough lines to know it *was* acting. I just couldn't figure out what she wanted. "I mean, you're my best friend and I was horrible to you. It like, wasn't even me. And I know I don't deserve it but Tristan, I am *so* sorry."

She touched my cheek with her cold fingers. "Let's go back to the way it was. Our sleepovers, practicing choreography. Maybe what should have been."

Then, without warning, she leaned in and pressed her lips against mine. My chest got tight with the kiss, but this time it wasn't from affection or wanting. This time, it was from disgust. I pushed her back.

"Don't touch me," I said. "I'm with Keisha."

"But isn't this what you want? What you always wanted?"

"No, actually," I said. "I want Keisha."

Heather's face twisted up. It still didn't seem quite sincere. "Why can't you just forgive me?" she pleaded. "I need you. You're my best friend. I *need* you to work with me. Backstage, onstage, we could be a dynamite couple."

I touched my lips and looked at Heather. For a moment, she looked sweet and kind, the way Heather did for our four years of our friendship. For a moment, I wondered whether it was just in my head, whether she really was acting.

But then I thought about the weeks of cruelty. About Robbie's second and third suicide attempts. About Heather turning Durrell on me, turning the team on me. Thought about the way she got the guys to destroy my locker, betrayed my confidence, made Robbie decide to out himself before he was ready to—just so he could right her wrong, just so he could protect me.

I took a deep breath, and stepped away from her. Shook my head. "I'm sorry, Heather. I don't think I can."

"Tristan—"

She extended her arms to me, but I turned my back to her and walked toward the stage door.

"Tristan!" Heather's desperate plea was accompanied by sobbing. I hesitated. I considered turning back, about saying, "Okay I forgive you, but this is your last chance." I lingered, shifting my weight from side to side before I saw him.

I don't know how he got backstage, but there was my twin, standing maybe twenty feet from me, congratulatory flowers clutched in one hand. He stood still, but in my head, I could see him shaking, scared, waiting for something, for me. Like he wanted to protect me but still needed some sort of protection. It would be a long road to recovery, but now, instead of going alone, Robbie was looking for someone to guide him through dangerous territory. More specifically, he was looking for *me*. I was younger than him by fourteen minutes, but I was his hero. I was team captain. Robbie looked up to me. Always did, but I was too jealous to realize it until now. Robbie wanted me to lead him through life, and I was okay with that. I'd stay by his side, not from obligation, but respect, love. I'd be there when Robbie came to me in the night. When he would cry, I would pull him close to me, hum a little in his ear, sing something from a musical I liked. I would be there for the good times, blanket pulled over our heads as he'd whisper about *real* kisses and Raiden. I'd be there for him at draft day, squeezing his hand as each GM would make their selection until his name was called. I would go to his playoff games and scream louder than anyone when he scored or got an assist, or got in a fight with anyone who dared call him "queer." I would be there for him when the trial about Jimmy came up, testifying the truth, letting the world know how good a person Robbie was, how scared we were, how we almost died.

I would be his best friend, his brother, his twin.

My fists bunched up. I looked over my shoulder. Heather stood waiting, begging me to turn back the clock, to go back to the time when we were the only people who mattered in our own world of musicals and fan-fiction and pretending we were someone else. That we were the only two people in the world that mattered.

Slowly, I approached Robbie. I felt like I was dragging something heavy with each step.

Is everything okay? he asked without speaking out loud.

I looked over my shoulder once more; Heather was still standing in the wings, waiting, watching.

Yeah, it's fine.

Together, we walked to the stage door. Outside, our friends and family and castmates would be waiting. The whole hockey team and our parents. Raiden. Keisha.

I put my hand on the door, then hesitated.

You don't have to, Robbie said in my head.

I know, I thought, before I pulled it open. Robbie stepped out into the cheers first, leaving me to close Heather and the memories of the nothing Robbie and I used to be out of our lives.

ACKNOWLEDGMENTS

I'm incredibly grateful to the people who made *Jerkbait*—and my dream of becoming an author—possible.

My editor, McKelle George: thank you for your unending patience and willingness to explain things, repeatedly, until I "got it." I possibly drove you nuts along the way with my questions, but your willingness to explain really helped me.

The entire Jolly Fish Press team, especially Chris, Zach, Alexis, Kayla, Kelsy, TJ, and Reece. From the bottom of my heart, THANK YOU.

My amazing agent, Travis Pennington. To have you believe in *Jerkbait* from its first paragraph meant everything to me. Thank you for always having my back.

My wonderful family, you have stuck with me through the hard times and never let me give up on my dreams, no matter what they were. I might not have been able to make the Olympics, but becoming an author is equally satisfying, perhaps even more so as now I'm much more human.

My Goddard family, I tear up any time I think of you, your amazing words, your wisdom, and your, "YOU CAN DO IT!" You taught me how to turn the competition off and become a better person, and, in turn, a much better writer.

Kale Night, my best friend, my chupacabra, the Eiri to my Tohma. You saved me from a dark place with a Sigur Rós album and encouraged me to become a novelist when I was lost.

David Williamson, my fiancé, my beta, my confidant, thank

you for making me re-evaluate what I needed to do, the last kick in the ass I needed so I could succeed, and your willingness to help me, especially with the musical research.

Additional thanks to Mark Spencer, David Galef, Cat Ide, and Traci Dolan-Priestley for taking time out to help me, whether it was through discussing concept, editing, proofreading, or taking a chance on a (then) stranger.

A special thanks to the You Can Play organization, especially Patrick Burke and Anna Aagenes. Your support for LGBTQ athletes is changing—and saving—lives. This shout-out extends to all of the professional athletes who are standing up for equality.

And last, but not least, I thank you, the readers, for your support. The tweets and FB messages and blog posts have really helped encourage me to continue as I eagerly work on my next novel. Writing is an often thankless task; each word of encouragement lights a candle on the way to the end of the tunnel.

MIA SIEGERT received her MFA from Goddard College and her undergraduate degree from Montclair State University, where she won Honorable Mention in the 2009 English Department Awards for Fiction. Mia has been published in Clapboard House, Word Riot, The Limn Literary & Arts Journal, as well as a few other small presses. A short reading of *Jerkbait* was performed by the New Jersey Playwrights Association where it was tremendously received. Mia currently works as an adjunct professor and a costume designer, most recently having finished a production of *Cats*, featuring Ken Page, the original Broadway Old Deuteronomy.

ABOUT YOU CAN PLAY

YOU CAN PLAY is a non-profit organization whose mission is to ensure safety and inclusion for all who participate in sports, including LGBT athletes, coaches, and fans. You Can Play believes sports teams should focus on the athlete's skills, work ethic, and competitive spirit, not their sexual orientation, gender identity, or gender expression.

You Can Play works to guarantee that athletes are given a fair opportunity to compete, judged by other athletes and fans alike, only by what they contribute to the sport or their team's success. You Can Play also seeks to challenge the culture of locker rooms and spectator areas by focusing only on an athlete's skills, work ethic and competitive spirit.

In 2012, You Can Play was launched by Patrick Burke of the NHL along with Brian Kitts, a sports marketing and entertainment executive, and Glenn Witman of GForce Sports. Brendan Burke, the brother of Patrick Burke and son of Brian Burke, a longtime NHL executive, made international headlines when he came out as gay in 2009. A few months after he came out, Brendan died in a car accident. You Can Play was founded in Brendan Burke's honor.

Website: www.youcanplayproject.org
Twitter: @YouCanPlayTeam
Contact: brian@youcanplayproject.org